TOUGH
stuff

KIRSTY MURRAY

Pictures by

Harry Harrison

For Billy
who has made a lot of tough stuff
bearable for everyone around him

Copyright © text, Kirsty Murray 1999
© illustrations, Harry Harrison 1999

**Teaching notes for *Tough Stuff* can be found on the
Allen & Unwin website: see address below**

First published in 1999 by
Allen & Unwin Pty Ltd
9 Atchison Street
St Leonards NSW 1590
Australia
Phone: (61 2) 8425 0100
Fax: (61 2) 9906 2218
E-mail: frontdesk@allen-unwin.com.au
Web: http://www.allen-unwin.com.au

10 9 8 7 6 5 4 3 2 1

National Library of Australia
cataloguing-in-publication data:

Murray, Kirsty.

     Tough stuff.

     Includes index.
     ISBN 1 86448 929 4

     1. Heroes - Juvenile literature. 2 Children - Juvenile literature.
     I. Harrison, Harry, 1965-. II. Title.

A820.80352054

Designed by Sandra Nobes
Set in Sabon and Arbitrary
Printed in Australia by Australian Print Group, Maryborough, Vic.

Kirsty Murray was born in Australia but spent her teenage years in Canada before travelling the world and living all over the place. She has worked in dozens of different occupations from forest ranger to artist, model and teacher. Eventually she realised she wasn't cut out for any of these exotic jobs or locations and settled down in Melbourne as a full-time writer. *Tough Stuff* is her third book for Allen & Unwin, following *Man-eaters and Blood-suckers* and *Howard Florey Miracle Maker*.

Kirsty lives in a chaotic household with her husband and their gang of six kids. They all think she's pretty tough and she's hoping it stays that way. Once they've worked out what a pushover she is, she'll be in big trouble.

ACKNOWLEDGEMENTS

Unearthing the stories in this book proved to be one of the biggest adventures I've ever been on. Thanks to all those who helped me on the journey, especially Walter Rutkowski of the Carnegie Hero Fund Commission, Sue Cutler of the Royal Humane Society of Australasia, Magnus Bergmar, and Ron Adams at Broad Meadows Middle School for advice and resources; Ruby Hunter and Eva (Weiss) Slonim for permission to tell their stories; Sally Rogow, Steven Vitto of the New York Holocaust Museum, Juliet O'Connor and the State Library of Victoria for invaluable leads and encouragement; David, William and Matthew Taft for priceless feedback; Ken Harper and the Murray-Harper Bunch for going the distance.

Organisations that contributed ideas and material include: Amnesty International, Free the Children, Community Aid Abroad, The Nizkor Project, The Jewish Memorial Museum and Library (Melbourne), and The Royal Humane Society of NSW. Those I've overlooked, please forgive me.

Special thanks to Ros Price for her good faith, Sarah Brenan for her tireless help in making the whole thing work, and Harry Harrison, for sticking with the project as it metamorphosed.

The following authors provided primary sources for the Holocaust stories: Martin Gilbert, *The Boys* (Arek's story); Eva Fogelman, *Conscience and Courage: Rescuers of Jews During the Holocaust* (Stefania and Helena's story); Paul Valent, *Child Survivors* (Eva's story); and also the very incredible *The Anthology of Armed Jewish Resistance* edited by Isaac Kowalski (Paul's story).

CHECK THIS OUT FIRST

Hi, my name's Milo.
I was named after a really famous hero who won heaps of prizes for wrestling at some Olympic Games in Ancient Greece. I used to think it was pretty hard for a scrawny kid like me to live up to a name like that, until I started finding out more about what heroes are really like. Some people reckon heroes are all big muscly blokes, but that's comic-book stuff. In the real world all kinds of people are heroes, including kids.

A lot of grown-ups think kids should be seen and not heard. Suits me. I get a lot of great stories for my collection from just hanging around and listening. Some kids collect stamps, comics, Warhammer things, or whatever. Me, I collect stories.

I have this incredible memory—like a big shed. Every corner is crammed full of stuff; a shed/head full of stories. Check out the pic to see how my brain works—crowded or what?

A lot of people reckon history is all about adult stuff, but every grown-up was a kid once. The fact is, you don't have to grow up to make your mark on the world. I've got the stories to prove it—stories about extraordinary kids and about ordinary kids who have done amazing things.

Sometimes when I tell one of my stories, people say—'You're kidding' and I say, 'No, it's true—I kid you not!' The thing is, all my stories are true. Fairy-tales and all that sort of thing are okay for some, but I like the real stuff—the tough stuff.

When times are good and grown-ups behave themselves, kids aren't put to the test too much. But when the going gets tough, they show the world that they can really cut it.

So here's a swag of some of my stories—true stories about real kids and how they handle the tough stuff.

MiLO

1 RESCUERS

CHEATING DEATH, CHANGING FATE, SAVING LIVES

Coming to the rescue and especially saving a life makes you a hero in everyone's books; but being brave doesn't mean not being scared. Kid rescuers are just ordinary kids who out of the blue did something extraordinary.

All the kids in this chapter won awards for their bravery, either from the government or from the various organisations that give prizes for heroism. But the real prize for each of them was knowing that they had saved someone's life.

Billy and the bull

Billy Corcoran was only nine years old but he was already pretty useful around the farm that his family owned in Amphitheatre, Victoria. When his dad, Greg, asked him to help sort some cattle at a neighbour's house, he was keen to go.

It was a windy day in the early spring of 1994. They

took the company car and reached the neighbour's cattle yard around 4.30 p.m. Their job was to separate the bulls from the steers, so that the neighbour could send some away to be sold.

Greg sent Billy off to collect some sticks to use in herding the cattle between pens, while he climbed into the yards. He opened the gate between the pens, a steer bumped it and the gate slammed Greg hard in the back, making him stumble forward. A bull, alarmed by the sudden movement, charged him.

Billy heard his dad shout, and ran towards the pens.

'Watch out, Billy!' cried Greg as the huge bull bore down on top of him, and rammed him with its head.

As he struggled to avoid the angry bull's hooves, Greg discovered he couldn't move his legs. He was paralysed from the waist down. In the same moment, he saw a flash of blond hair and realised Billy was still racing towards him, inside the pen.

'Run, Billy. Get out, Billy. Get out of here!' he screamed.

But Billy had other ideas. He beat the bull across the back and head with his sticks, driving it away from his dad's body.

'You get out of here. Clear off!' Billy shouted, thrashing the bull as hard as he could.

When the bull withdrew, Billy handed a stick to Greg to protect himself with. He raced across the yard to open the gate, planning to drive the bull into a neighbouring pen. But the minute Billy's back was turned, the crazy animal set to again.

Billy was across the yard and on the attack again in a flash. Like a mad bull-terrier he rushed at the huge animal, giving it a painful blow across its eye. His head didn't even reach the top of the animal's back but he attacked it so fiercely that the stick he was using splintered and broke in his hands. The bull backed off and Billy herded it out of the yard with his hands, shouting and clapping to shoo it into the adjoining pen. Finally, he swung the gate shut and raced back to his dad.

Greg Corcoran's face was the colour of white-ash. Billy knelt beside him and rested a hand on his shoulder.

'I can't move, Billy,' said Greg. 'I haven't got any feeling in my legs.'

'Don't worry, Dad. Everything will be okay. I'll take care of you.'

Billy had heard that after bad accidents people go into shock and his dad was looking pretty bad. Greg closed his eyes for a moment and Billy could see he was struggling with the pain.

Billy ran back to the car and grabbed the mobile phone from the front seat, plus a coat and blanket from the back.

'Now, Dad,' he said as he draped a blanket over Greg, 'you have to show me how to use this thing so I can call Mum.'

He crouched down and followed the instructions that his father haltingly gave him.

The call to his mum was brief. She would contact the ambulance and be over as quickly as she could. Meanwhile, Billy was in charge.

'You have to keep warm, Dad,' he said as he climbed under the blanket with him. 'A bloke came and talked to us about hypothermia at school. When you've had an accident, your body gets really shocked and you get really cold. I know what I'm doing. I'm gonna give you lots of cuddles to warm you up.'

The rain came before help arrived. Billy checked out a nearby shed and found an old horse blanket. Using the sticks he had gathered, he built a shelter over Greg to keep the rain off and then hopped back under the blankets to keep his dad warm.

It took over half an hour for help to arrive. After Billy's dad was loaded into the ambulance, Billy got behind the wheel of his father's car and drove it over to a neighbour's house, following his mum who was in the car ahead of him.

No one was as surprised as Billy when the newspaper reporters turned up on his doorstep and started making a fuss over him.

'So why did you do it, Billy?' they asked.

'Cause I love my dad,' he answered, amazed that grown-ups could ask such a stupid question.

Country kids seem to be pretty good at rescuing— working in the great outdoors with their parents, driving tractors and handling machinery or animals means they're put to the test more often than city kids.

Sometimes the main thing you need is persistence: that means hanging in there and staying brave when all you want to do is give up. The next story is about just that kind of courage.

Lean on me

Once a week Colleen Cooke and her dad, Kim, saddled their horses and headed up the mountainside together. Colleen and her mum and dad lived in Victor, Idaho, just west of the Grand Teton range. Although she was only nine years old, Colleen was an expert rider. Heading out for a long ride with her dad had to rate as one of her favourite things.

It was springtime—30 May 1987—but the air was still cold and crisp. There was even a bit of snow left high in the mountains. Colleen watched her dad saddle up the new filly—a skittish three-year-old that shied away as he loaded her up. He stroked the horse's neck to calm it before swinging into the saddle.

They set out on a forestry road before turning into the forest and heading up the mountain. On a high ridge six kilometres from home they climbed off their horses and settled down on a boulder to admire the view.

'Thirsty, honey?' asked Colleen's dad.

'You bet,' she replied.

'I've got some soda in the saddlebags. I'll grab a couple for us.'

Colleen gazed out over the valley. There was an odd swishing noise behind her and she turned to see her dad rolling over on the ground. He rose to his knees, clutching his head, with blood pouring through his fingers.

'Dad! Dad!' she cried as she ran to him.

A kick from the filly's hooves had caved in the upper right side of Kim's head. Colleen put her hands on her father's shoulders and looked at his injury. A gaping hole with fragments of bone and exposed brain was where her father's right eye had been. She felt sick.

Colleen took a deep breath and kept her voice steady.

'Looks like you're hurt bad. I'm going to have to go for help, Dad, but everything will be okay. You just rest here awhile. I'll be back real soon.'

Colleen ran to her pony and swung into the saddle. She began the long steep journey back down the mountain, but as she looked down through the thick stand of pine and aspen, she realised she wasn't sure which way to go. Her dad knew the mountain like the back of his hand, but without him to guide her she could easily get lost—and if she got lost, what would happen to him? What if she got back okay and then couldn't find where she'd left him?

Twice she changed her direction and then turned her horse around and headed back towards her dad.

'Don't leave him,' came a voice as she rode down the mountain for the third time.

It wasn't her own voice, but one that kept on echoing inside her head as she rode. She reined in her horse and prayed that the decision she was about to make would be the right one. Then she turned and headed back up the mountain.

She knelt beside her father, trying to remember every piece of first aid advice she'd ever heard. First she checked his breathing. Then she scooped some snow from the shadow of a boulder, pressed it to her father's face, and gently wiped away some of the blood.

'Dad. We're going home—together. And I know we're going to make it. I know because I prayed.'

Kim Cooke was barely conscious but Colleen's voice brought him round.

'Dad. You've got to come with me.'

'I haven't got the strength to stay in the saddle, Colleen.'

'That's okay, Dad. We'll walk. I can help you. We've just got to get to the forestry road. We've got to get out of the woods.'

Holding the reins of her pony in one hand, Colleen helped her dad to his feet and hooked her other arm around his waist.

'Just lean on my shoulder, Dad. Lean on me all you like and we'll make it okay.'

After only 30 metres, Kim slumped to the ground and vomited. He was nearly blacking out from pain. But Colleen wouldn't let him lie down. She knew she had to keep him conscious and she had to keep him moving. Slowly, slowly, they made their way down the mountainside.

It took hours to go less than a few kilometres. She knew he was close to dying but she couldn't afford to panic.

Five hours after leaving the ridge, they neared the foot of the mountain. The forestry road was within sight. She guided Kim to a spot on the edge of the roadway and he lowered himself down against a fallen tree trunk.

'Promise you'll wait right here,' she said. 'I'll be back with help. I'll be back so fast you won't even notice I was gone.'

Colleen mounted her pony and headed for home at a gallop.

'Please, God, don't let it be too late—don't let Dad die.'

She put her head down and urged the horse on. Her dad's riderless horse had followed her and now it galloped ahead, streaking towards home.

Soon, she could make out the sound of a car engine racing towards her. It was her Uncle Casey—when her father's riderless horse had turned into the yard, he'd leapt into the four-wheel drive and headed out to investigate.

'It's Dad,' she yelled. 'He's up by the beaver dam on the side of the road.'

Kim was taken by ambulance to hospital. Surgeons worked all night to repair the damage to his skull. Hardly a bone in his face was intact and his right eye had to be removed but, incredibly, he suffered no brain damage. He was back on the mountain by August of that year.

When people said how brave Colleen had been, she answered simply, 'When we were up on the mountain, it wasn't a matter of whether to be brave or not. I just knew I couldn't let my dad die.'

Saving someone you love sort of makes sense—risking your life for someone you've never met is something else again.

The kid in the next story won a Carnegie Medal for Bravery. You can't get this medal for rescuing a member of your family because the people who award it figure that's a natural thing to do. Mostly they don't award it to kids either, because they reckon that kids don't know how much danger they're in when they save people. But the boy in this next story knew exactly what he was up to.

In the nick of time

Joe Terry wasn't all that interested in babies, but he never forgot the day he met one-year-old Ygzeña Gallegos in August 1995.

Joe was 15 years old and lived on R Street in Merced, California, opposite the railway line. On a lazy summer evening, Joe was lounging around on his front porch listening to his Walkman when he noticed a tiny kid—a baby—sitting on the tracks.

Ygzeña's house, like Joe's, was opposite the railway line. Ygzeña (Jenny for short) and her three-year-old brother Josh had been playing in their front yard. Somehow, the two toddlers had managed to unlatch the front gate and slip off for a stroll down the railway tracks without anyone realising what they were up to. They'd wandered along the line until Jenny's tiny legs were too tired to take her further. While Josh collected rocks, Jenny sat down on a long stretch of shiny silver track.

As Joe stared in surprise he heard the long whistle of the 8.25 train. It was heading out of town, roaring south at over 100 km per hour. Joe saw it all happening at once—the baby on the track, the silver train streaking towards her—and all of a sudden Joe was running. It was the longest 100-metre dash he'd ever made in his life. He darted through four lanes of traffic and ran up the slope towards the tracks. People hung out of their car windows and yelled at him, 'Hey, kid, get off the tracks, there's a train coming!'

Joe ignored them. He leapt on to the tracks, knocked the little boy out of the way and made straight for the baby. Her chubby legs swung into the air as he swept her up into his arms. The train bore down on top of them and Joe caught a glimpse of the horrified expression on the driver's face. Joe's baseball hat blew off his head and he felt the wind from the train skim along his back as he clasped the baby to his chest and jumped.

The driver of the train was shaking as he hit the emergency brake. He was convinced he had just wiped out an entire family. But by the time he and the conductor got out to check, Joe had already taken Josh by the hand and led the two kids back to their home.

Mostly, little kids need big people to watch out for them. But being little doesn't mean you're stupid. Sometimes even really young kids can come to the rescue.

This babe is wise

It was quiet around the house when Nicola's big brothers had gone off to school and kindergarten; but being all of two and a half years old, Nicola could keep pretty busy just chatting to herself. Sometimes she'd sing little ditties, like 'Ready set go—phone 000.' Mum was always telling the big boys that one.

Nicola was singing to herself when she heard a crash in the kitchen. She toddled down the hall to investigate. Her mum was lying on the floor in a funny position. Nicola squatted down next to her and patted her.

'Mummy,' she said loudly. 'Mummy, wake up. Don't go sleep!'

Nicola's mum didn't answer, so Nicola gave her another pat. Then she hugged her and spoke very loudly right into her ear.

'Mummy! Wake up!'

Nicola knew something wasn't right, and she knew what you had to do when you needed help.

'Ready, set, go—phone 000,' she sang as she marched into the hall. But the phone was mounted high up on a wall—even on her tiptoes, Nicola couldn't reach it. She stamped back into the kitchen and started wrestling with a chair. It took a long time to get that chair through the doorway. Nicola could hardly see over the seat—it was twice her size. Eventually, she managed to drag and push it down the hall. She felt hot and bothered, but she clambered up onto the chair and reached for the phone.

'000,' she sang as she hit the button three times.

A nice lady was suddenly on the other end of the line, talking to her.

'She can't wake up,' said Nicola.

'Who can't wake up, darling?' asked the lady on the other end.

'Mummy,' said Nicola.

'Your mummy can't wake up?'

'No.'

'Do you know where you live, sweetie?'

Most two-year-olds wouldn't have a clue, but Nicola

knew the lot. She gave the lady her address. She even knew the phone number.

Pretty soon, a couple of men in an ambulance turned up. Nicola couldn't open the front door for them so they came around the back and Nicola rode to the hospital with her mum and the ambulance men.

Racing against the clock

 It turned out Nicola's mum had suffered an allergic reaction to a painkiller that the doctor had given her to help with the pain in a broken shoulder. The drug had made her black out. If Nicola hadn't come to the rescue when she did, her mum could have been in really serious danger. When it comes to saving lives, time and how you use it can be the most important part of the rescue, and sometimes there's only a split second to make the right decision.

The fastest five seconds of your life

Stephen Jury loosened his tie and shifted from one foot to the other. His mum had yelled at him about making sure he was on time for his first day at a new school, and his new uniform felt tight and too hot. It was going to be another stinking hot day.

It was the first day of the school year for 1983. Stephen was waiting on Boronia railway station for the next train to the city, along with 200 other people.

Stephen didn't know the man standing a few metres away from him but he knew what to do when that man suddenly passed out and fell from the platform—smack onto the railway tracks, just as the 8.10 train to the city came roaring into the station. The train was only 100 metres away and moving at over 60 kph. Stephen had five seconds to save a life.

He jumped. 'C'mon mister, please mister,' Stephen muttered as he hooked his hands under the man's arms and tried to yank him up. But it was no good—and the train was hurtling at them. He rolled the man towards the platform wall and threw himself on top.

The train driver saw the man lying unconscious, the boy in his school uniform leaping down onto the tracks. He slammed on the emergency brakes and blew the train whistle—a long scream blasting into the morning air.

Back on the platform, there was panic and confusion. The stationmaster tried to clear the crowd away, but some people were boarding the train, oblivious to what had happened. Others were running up and down trying to see what had become of the boy and the man. A woman was crying. A baby screamed. The stationmaster and the distressed train driver shouted at people to get out of the way. They uncoupled the rear carriages and slowly moved the front three forward, dreading what they might find.

The stationmaster climbed down to find Stephen lying on top of the man with his back to the wall. There was only a 30-40 cm space between the wheels and the platform, but Stephen had managed to wedge both himself and the man into it cleanly. Stephen looked up at the stationmaster and smiled.

The man was lifted onto the platform and taken to hospital, where he was treated for cuts and bruises. Stephen sat on the platform and ran his hand through his hair. His new uniform was rumpled and one of his shoes had been torn off by the train.

'Can I have my shoe back?' he asked. 'I don't want to be late for school. It's my first day, you know.'

They found his missing shoe on the tracks and Stephen caught the next train to school.

Star of courage

Later that day when he phoned his mum, Stephen didn't tell her about the accident. He was worried she'd be cross with him if he 'fessed up to being late for school. Stephen's mum was anything but cross when, later in the same year, he was awarded the Australian Star of Courage and two gold medals from the Royal Humane Society for his heroism.

2 BRAINBOXES

You'd think that being a genius would make life a bowl of cherries, but being different is never easy, and being extra smart can really set you apart from the rest of the world. When you read about the brainboxes in this chapter you might reckon they're really extraordinary, but in the end they're just kids—not freaks.

Bidder at your bidding

George shifted from one foot to the other as the men from the university shuffled through their papers and frowned at him. Finally, a bearded professor cleared his throat and looked George in the eye.

'If a flea springs 2 feet 3 inches in every hop, how many hops must it take to go round the world, the circumference being 25 020 miles; and how long would it be performing the journey, allowing it to take 60 hops per minute without intermission?' asked the professor, stroking his beard.

Ten-year-old George tipped his head to one side and thought for a minute—70 seconds, to be exact. Then he smiled.

'58 713 600 hops, sir,' said George. 'And it would take 1 year, 314 days, 3 hours and 20 minutes.'

It all adds up

George Bidder was born in a small village in Devonshire in 1806. There were a lot of kids in his family and his dad wasn't a rich man, so George wasn't sent to school. Most days he would wander down to the blacksmith's to help in the forge. The blacksmith would give him odd jobs, and there were always people coming and going.

One day, a farmer who had come into the workshop to have some tools repaired began arguing with the blacksmith about the price. The two men added up the cost of the work but each came up with different answers.

'Excuse me, sir,' said George, 'Neither of you have the right answer. It comes to 2 pounds, 5 shillings and sixpence.'

The men looked at him in surprise and sat down to work out the cost again, only to discover that George was right.

'How did you work that one out, boy? You were very quick with the answer,' said the farmer.

'I like to count,' replied George.

'What's 13 times 17, then, lad?' asked the farmer

George sorted out the correct answer in a few seconds. The farmer scratched his head and looked at the blacksmith.

'Well, George,' asked the blacksmith, 'Can you tell us what 130 times 165 comes to?'

'I'm sorry sir,' said George 'I don't know what you call a number that's bigger than 999. Is there such a number, and if there is, what do you call it?'

'Why of course there is, lad. That's called a thousand,' answered the blacksmith.

'So 10 times 100 is called a thousand is it?'

'Yes, that's right.'

'Well, sir, 130 times 165 must be 21 450,' replied George.

The blacksmith and the farmer raised their eyebrows in astonishment. They quizzed George with endless questions and every time the boy answered in an instant.

Forging to fame

George's big brother had taught George how to count to ten when he was six years old and then how to get to 100. George worked the rest out for himself. He used his marble collection to help him. He kept them in a little cloth bag in his pocket and he'd squat on the ground outside the cottage and count them over and over again. As his passion for counting grew, he started to collect dried peas as well. One day, his father saw him kneeling in the dirt making patterns with his marbles and peas, and gave him a little bag of gunshot pellets to add to his game. The bag of shot was a fantastic treasure. He could lay it out in sets of five or ten or however he fancied.

Word spread about the boy at the forge, and people began to come to the blacksmith's especially to test his incredible abilities. George became the talk of the county.

Before long, George's dad had caught on to what a sensation his son was. He organised to take George on a tour of the country and George was billed as 'The Incredible Calculating Boy'. Sometimes they set up a tent, sometimes they staged a demonstration of George's skill in a local hall. People came from all across the country paid to hear him answer questions about numbers.

Easy peasy

In 1816 George was invited to Cambridge University to display his incredible ability to the university's top mathematicians.

After more than an hour of questions, one of them asked, 'Do you remember the first sum I gave you when you arrived?'

'Why yes, sir,' said George and ran the string of figures past the man again.

The men murmured in astonishment and continued with the questions.

'Divide 468 592 413 563 by 9076.'

It took George less than one minute to come up with the answer.

'It comes to 51 629 838,' said George, 'with a few thousand left over, sir, 'cause it doesn't quite fit.'

George never produced the wrong answer. In the days before calculators and computers, people could spend hours calculating sums. George was like a living calculating machine.

At the age of 11, George still couldn't write his numbers down. As a matter of fact, he couldn't write at all. No one had given him a formal lesson in anything in his whole life. After the Cambridge interview, he was sent to school and at last was taught how to read and write as well as how to write down the numbers that he added up so easily inside his head.

Rich men who were impressed by George's calculating ability offered to pay for his education. At 16, he won a prize from the University of Edinburgh which meant he could study mathematics and engineering there.

George grew up to become a successful engineer. He designed the London telegraphic system and built the Victoria Docks in London. He never lost his unusual ability to add figures—even as an old man he could instantly supply the answers to impossible sums. Two days before his death in 1878, a friend was trying to calculate how many vibrations of light the human eye received in one second.

'Put down your pencil—you don't need to work it out,' said old George. 'The answer is 444 433 651 200 000.'

Faster than lightning

George Bidder wasn't the first or the last 'lightning calculator' on record—over the centuries heaps of child prodigies have cropped up to amaze grown-ups with what they know. Zerah Colborn was an American boy, born in Vermont in 1801, who was a bit like George. He toured America to show what he could do. Eighty years earlier, another little tacker called Christian Friedrich Heinecken could add figures up at a fantastic speed by the time he was three, and he also spoke fluently in Latin, German  **and French. Christian only lived to be four years old but he knew a whole lot about world history, the basics of maths and all the main events in the Bible—at least that's what everybody reckons. But it seems pretty certain that the most amazing brainbox of them all was William James Sidis.**

Surprise, surprise

'I've got a big surprise for Daddy,' said Billy Sidis, rocking back on his heels and smiling at his mother. Billy was three years old and loved to surprise his parents, especially his dad.

'What sort of surprise, Billy?' asked his mum.

'It's for his birthday. I have a present for him, but I can't tell you what it is. When the people come for dinner, then you'll be surprised too.'

When the guests were sitting comfortably in the living room that evening, Billy slipped into the room lugging a fat book.

'Does anyone know Latin?' he asked.

'Yes, I know a little,' replied one of the guests.

'Here,' said the three-year-old, depositing the book in the lap of the surprised visitor. 'I can read this, I can translate it into English for you, let me show you.'

The book was called *Caesar's Gallic Wars* and was all in Latin. Proudly Billy read out the first page and then crowed with laughter.

'Oh Daddy, aren't you surprised! I taught myself last week, with a bunch of mother's old books. All by myself!'

There wasn't much Billy couldn't teach himself. Before he was six he had taught himself Russian, French, German and Hebrew, and later he added Turkish and Armenian to his collection.

April Genius' Day

William James Sidis was born on 1 April 1898, April Fool's Day, in New York City. Billy's mum and dad were both clever people but Billy was something else, and certainly no fool.

When Billy was six months old his parents gave him a set of alphabet blocks, and by his first birthday he had learnt how to spell. When his parents took him for walks in Central Park, kids would come and ask the pretty, fat, blue-eyed baby to count to 100. By the time he was eighteen months old he was reading the *New York Times* as he sat in his highchair in the family apartment. He'd toddle along the bookshelf and pull out any book on request for visitors. Before he was two he was reading every book he could lay his hands on and he taught himself to type on his dad's typewriter.

Billy wore his parents down with his endless questions. They bought him an encyclopedia so he could look up his own answers.

Billy's parents took him with them everywhere. With his plump pink cheeks and sandy blond hair, he made a big hit at dinner parties showing off his abilities. One of his favourite party tricks was reciting railroad and bus timetables to the astonished grown-ups.

Billy's parents gave him maps, a globe of the world and a calendar, and Billy learnt to calculate everything about days. Eventually he would design a perpetual calender that could show what day of the week a certain date is in any year. Billy also taught himself anatomy, so he could help his dad study for his medical exams.

Shortcuts through the schoolyard

When Billy was six, he was sent to school—which seemed a bit of a waste of time as he knew more than most of his teachers. When his mum went to pick him up on the first day he was teaching his teacher a new way to

do fractions. It took three days for him to get promoted
from the first to the third grade. He graduated from
Grade 7 six months later.

Too young for high school, Billy stayed at home and
decided to write a book. Between the ages of six and eight
he wrote at least four books; a textbook on anatomy, one
on astronomy and two on grammar. He also started to
invent a new language.

By the time he was seven and a half he had passed the
Harvard Medical School anatomy exam and the entrance
exam for the Massachusetts Institute of Technology.
(Harvard and MIT are two of the top universities in
America.) He was obviously more than ready for high
school—but was high school ready for him? He was eight
years old when he started at Brookline High. He barely
came up to the elbows of his classmates and he had to
stand on a stool to write problems on the blackboard.

The press had got wind of the boy prodigy and
followed him around the school trying to interview him.
Sensational articles about him began to appear in all the
newspapers and soon he was famous as the youngest high
school student in America. Not all the articles written
about him were kind—journalists made fun of him as a
weird freak of nature. A lot of people wanted to believe
that there was something wrong with a kid who was so
clever.

Hell at Harvard

By the time he had spent three months at high school,
Billy had completely worn out all his teachers. His dad
tried to enrol the nine-year-old at Harvard University, but
Harvard refused him—not because he wasn't clever
enough; he was just too little. Finally, when he was 11 the

University decided to take him on as a special student.

Mathematics became his favourite subject and in 1910 he gave a two-hour lecture to the Harvard Mathematical Club. His grasp of mathematics was advanced even for an adult.

When he was 13, Billy was sent to live at Harvard as a boarder. It was a terrible time for him. He was laughed at, teased and harassed. The jealous grown-up students made him the butt of practical jokes, and Billy was constantly humiliated. Young women would pretend they were in love with him and then laugh at him when he blushed and stammered with embarrassment. Young men would trip him up, jostle him in the corridors or make rude remarks when he tried to speak in class. On top of it all, Billy's family was Jewish and there was a lot of anti-Semitism (hatred of Jewish people) at Harvard. His parents organised for him to have his own apartment, but of course that meant he was lonely and isolated.

Billy went home for the weekends but the only joy in his week at university was the work itself. He studied Greek, mathematics, American history, astronomy and French. When he finished his first degree, he decided he wanted to become a lawyer but the situation at Harvard was becoming more difficult for him. Things finally came to a bad end when a gang of bullies caught up with him outside class and threatened to beat him up. Billy had had enough.

The young professor

Although he was only 17 years old, Billy got himself a job teaching mathematics at Rice University in Texas. He was younger than nearly all his students, which inevitably led to trouble.

Billy was a bit of a slob—he didn't want to cut his hair, he hated having to shave and he dressed sloppily. His own students picked on him for his odd manners, especially his shyness around girls. But the people who often played the meanest jokes on Billy were the press—newspaper articles appeared full of misinformation about him and reporters poked fun at everything he said and did. After eight months at Rice University, Billy gave up and went home to Boston to study law.

Billy found his haven in books. Books didn't judge him, didn't care how sloppy he was, didn't mind that he was shy and hadn't worked out how to talk to girls. Books were his real friends.

Billy was a big fan of public transport and spent a lot of time travelling on trams and buses around the city. He believed that people needed to share more, and so he became involved with groups promoting ideas about how to change the world for the better. On May Day in 1919 he was arrested for marching in a parade that was stopped by the police. His parents were furious with him, and Billy had a pretty difficult couple of years trying to break away from their disapproval and start his own life.

The prodigy grows up

Billy was kind and gentle. He was a pacifist: he thought it was wrong to hurt people and he didn't believe in war. He had a small group of friends who appreciated his unusual manners and ideas, but mostly he kept to himself.

When the newspapers tracked him down for comment he said, 'My only plan and purpose for the future is to live near Boston as much as possible and seek happiness in my own way.' And that is exactly what he did.

He collected transit tickets, got himself a job as a clerk, and lived a quiet life.

Adding up IQs

The experts reckon that Billy Sidis' IQ was somewhere between 250 and 300 (higher than Einstein's). 'IQ' stands for intelligence quotient—there are tests that you can do to measure it. A regular IQ ranges from 85 to 115 and only about 1 per cent of people in the world have an IQ of 135 or more. But IQ tests can only tell you about one sort of cleverness.

There's a Greek woman called Hypatia who was a universal genius. She was one of history's most brilliant mathematicians and that wasn't all she could do: she wrote poetry as well as books about ideas. But she was lucky (and probably pretty persistent). In the past, a lot of people thought trying to teach girls anything much was a waste of time. The Sidises didn't bother to help their really clever daughter anywhere near as much as they did Billy. People thought that girls only needed to know how to look after the men in their lives. But a lot of changes have happened in the world since then and there are plenty of girls out there who are taking advantage of them.

Queen of the chessboard

Judit tossed her long red hair to one side and smiled a tiny smile at her opponent. She touched each of her pieces and then made her move with ruthless precision. The man opposite sighed. He knew that he had lost the game and that he was going to have to change his opinion about women and chess. Even worse, his opponent wasn't even a woman—just a girl. The kid in front of him was only 15 years old and had recently become the youngest 'grandmaster' in chess history. In over 1000 years of chess playing, there had never been a champion like Judit Polgar.

Judit Polgar was born in Hungary in 1977, the youngest of three sisters. Her dad and mum believed that geniuses are made, not born; they knew their daughters could achieve anything with the right help. They decided to teach the girls at home rather than sending them to school, even though the local authorities were against it.

Zsuzsa, the eldest, was the first to get interested in chess. Her two little sisters, who were five and seven years younger than she was, would sit beside her fascinated as she challenged their dad to yet another game. Pretty soon all three of them were hooked.

Lazlo Polgar wasn't an expert chess player—at best he considered himself mediocre. His wife, Klara, didn't play at all. But they could both see that their three girls had a gift for the game, especially Judit. She would spend up to ten hours at the chessboard studying all the possible moves that could be made. After years of practice she could calculate the result of any potential move at lightning speed and almost instantly make the right decision.

In 1984, the three sisters began attending international tournaments together with at least one of their parents. They were 14, nine and seven. Zsuzsa quickly became rated as the top woman chess player in the world but Judit took the spot away from her big sister in 1989 when she was 13, and she has kept it ever since. From then on, Judit refused to compete on the women's chess circuit and began to compete exclusively against men.

In 1991 Judit and Zsuzsa both attained the position of grandmaster. It was a stunning achievement—fewer than 1 per cent of grandmasters are female. At 15 years and 5 months of age, Judit was the youngest grandmaster in history, even younger than the legendary world champion Bobby Fischer had been when he earned the title in 1958. In 1993 she caused another sensation when she defeated former world champion Boris Spassky.

At a Rome Open chess tournament, Zsofia, the middle sister, registered one of the greatest individual performances in chess history. She won eight of nine games and in the ninth, her opponent could only force a draw. In 1997 Zsofia was ranked the sixth top female player in the world.

The game of life

Judit spends several months of the year travelling the world to compete in world-class chess competitions. She considers chess more than a hobby—it's her job and her passion. Whether she wins or loses a game, for Judit the excitement lies in taking risks, daring her opponent and herself to conquer the chessboard.

Judit Polgar isn't world champion yet—most people hit their peak ability when they're in their thirties—but she's on her way. A longtime friend and fellow grandmaster of chess, Alex Sherzer, said of Judit, 'She has the talent to be world champion some day. She has a very aggressive, dangerous style, she's one of the fastest players I've seen and she is afraid of nothing.'

3 FERALS

WILD AND MYSTERIOUS

WILD CHILD

For one reason or another, all sorts of backyard and barnyard animals—cats, dogs, pigs, even chooks—sometimes give up on hanging out with humans and go bush; go feral. It's pretty amazing, though, to think that kids have lived that way.

Feral kids might look like the opposite of brainboxes, but even if they don't know a lot about words and numbers, they know the world in a different way. I reckon they must be big on using all their senses just to survive. They've shown that even with all the odds stacked against them, kids can be pretty tough.

Out of the forest

The boy sat in a tree, watching one of the villagers take firewood into his cottage. The villager's garden had neat rows of root vegetables, and a walnut tree grew beside the stone wall. The boy ran across the cold hard ground to the garden and began foraging for potatoes or a walnut or two. It was mid-winter and he was starving. Absorbed in the search, he didn't notice a man approach.

'Wild child!' cried the man, swooping down and grabbing the boy by the arm.

Wild boy of Aveyron

The local commissioner, Constans-Saint-Estève, hurried through the village to the tanner's house. Everyone in Aveyron village was talking of the wild boy that the tanner had caught in his garden. As the commissioner, Constans-Saint-Estève decided it was his responsibility to do something about the strange newcomer.

Constans tried to get the boy to talk to him but the wild child just ignored him and went on staring into the fire, rocking back and forward on his heels. He was about 12 years old, thin and wiry, and except for the remains of a tattered shirt he was completely naked. His brown hair hung in a tangled mane down his back. His skin was dirty and covered in sores and scars.

The commissioner eventually managed to coax the boy to come home with him. Early the next morning he arranged for local police to take the boy to an orphanage in the town of Saint-Affrique while the authorities decided what to do with him.

The wild boy spent a miserable month in the orphanage. He spat out the soft white bread the staff fed him, and when they dressed him he tore the clothes off his body. He hated the beds, the walls and the way people stared at him. Within weeks every newspaper in Paris was running stories about the 'Savage of Aveyron'. Rumours sprang up that he was hairy and vicious and that he could jump from tree to tree like a squirrel. Meanwhile, the boy lay whimpering in a corner of the orphanage, longing for the forest.

A friend in need

A priest named Bonnaterre expressed an interest in the boy and made a written application to look after him. When he brought the boy back to his village, Rodez, a huge crowd pressed around to stare. In frustration, the wild boy bit anyone who came too close.

Parents who had lost their children came to see if the boy was theirs, but in five months at Rodez, no one laid claim to him. The priest was busy with other work and it was the gardener of the school, a man called Clair, who cared for the boy.

One day the priest decided to take the boy on a visit to a friend in the country. Now that he was clean, the boy looked anything but wild. He had delicate white skin, a round, agreeable face and long eyelashes. Yet his old habits were strong. He wasn't the least interested in the other guests, but found the table laden with food really exciting—he set to, stuffing as much food into his mouth as he could. When he had eaten his fill, he swept the leftovers into his shirt and went out to bury them in a corner of the garden. The priest realised that educating the wild child was going to be a long and gruelling job.

The wilds of Paris

The boy grew fat in his time at Rodez. He loved to be tickled, and laughed easily. When he had come in from the woods he wasn't housebroken but Clair managed to persuade him to go outside when he needed to, though he still had no modesty. In August, Clair and Bonnaterre took him to the famous Institute for the Deaf and Dumb in Paris, where he would supposedly be helped by the best doctors in France. Clair was sorry to part from him and said he would be happy to take the boy back if no one wanted him. They left Paris assuming that he would be well cared for.

But no one came to treat him; no one took responsibility for his care. By November, the boy had lost his sweetness. What manners Clair had taught him were gone. He couldn't bear the endless stream of visitors who came to stare at him. His attendants fastened a leash to his waist to walk him around the grounds for exercise. The rest of the time he lay in his own filth, refusing to be washed. He grew to hate everyone, biting and scratching anyone who came near him. The famous doctors who had been interested in him at a distance were disgusted by him up close. No one was willing to take on the job of teaching the wild boy how to live with humans.

Dr Itard

There was one young doctor at the Institute who wasn't prepared to give up on the wild boy. Jean-Marc Gaspard Itard was only 25 years old but he managed to talk the heads of the institute into letting him try to teach the boy whom everyone else thought was unteachable. A nurse, Madame Guérin, was hired to care for the boy's daily needs, and Dr Itard set to work.

One day, Dr Itard noticed that the boy looked up and grunted with pleasure whenever anybody made the sound 'o'. Usually he ignored conversation that went on around him. Itard named him 'Victor' (in French, the 'r' is almost silent) so that every time his name was spoken, the boy would smile.

Itard quickly established that the boy wasn't deaf. In fact, there didn't seem to be anything amiss with him physically. He had a thick scar about 5 cm long on his neck, as if someone had once tried to cut it, but this hadn't affected his ability to make sounds. The problem was that the only thing he was interested in was food. Victor seemed to spend most of his day thinking about the next thing he was going to eat. He stole food and hid it in his room. Many people supposed Victor had lived with wolves, but the boy preferred to eat vegetarian—nuts and root vegetables were his favourite, preferably raw, but any piece of fruit or dry snack would do.

Dr Itard spent several hours every day trying to teach Victor how to talk, read and write. There seemed no reason why Victor shouldn't learn to speak, but he was not the most willing student. Teacher and pupil would often be at loggerheads, Victor refusing to co-operate and Dr Itard refusing to give up. When the pressure got too much for Victor, he would throw the cardboard letters on the floor and storm out of the room in disgust. But the more Victor resisted, the more determined Dr Itard was that he should continue.

Victor's fits of rage grew more violent. He would bite the mantelpiece and throw things around the room—even burning coals from the fireplace. At the height of his tantrum he would lie on the floor and thrash around until he passed out.

Dr Itard was worried that Victor would injure himself and feared that if the fits continued all their good work would be undone. He decided he had to do something to shock Victor into stopping his tantrums.

One day, he noticed Victor was afraid of heights. The next time Victor started writhing on the floor, Dr Itard grabbed him around the hips, flung the window open and held him half out the window. It was five storeys down to a stone pavement. Victor went limp with terror. When Dr Itard hauled him back inside, Victor quietly returned to his work. Afterwards, he lay on his bed and wept. It was the first time Dr Itard reduced Victor to tears. It wouldn't be the last.

Lessons end

At the end of five years of intense work, Victor knew only 100 words. He was no closer to being able to read or write, although he could spell *lait* (French for milk). He still preferred to spend most of his time alone. The boy was becoming increasingly unhappy and Dr Itard felt he could do no more. He decided it would be best to leave Victor with his nurse, Madame Guérin.

With Madame Guérin, Victor could at last be himself. She had taught him to drink milk and loved him with a tenderness that asked nothing of him in return. The French government paid a pension to Madame Guérin and she cared for Victor to the end of his days. He died in 1828, aged 40. He had never learnt to talk properly and the only sign that he had once been wild was the excitement he showed at the rising of the full moon, the first snowfalls or the howling of the south wind.

The quiet path

If a kid like Victor came out of a forest today, doctors would probably say he was 'autistic'. For kids with autism, being in the world can seem like getting snowed under by an avalanche of information. They have to shut down and go deep into themselves just to survive.

Focusing on small things and basic routines helps them find a quiet path in a world that's full of confusion.

Although Dr Itard didn't manage to teach Victor everything he wanted to, lots of people read his books and some of his methods have been used by people working with kids with all sorts of problems, including autistic kids. In some ways, Victor probably taught Itard more than Itard taught Victor. Through working with Victor, Dr Itard came to understand some really important things about how people learn.

The ghosts of Godamuri

'Reverend Singh, please sir. Two *manush-bagha* (man-ghosts) are living in the jungle near here—about seven miles from the village. You must help us get rid of these things. Will you help us kill these ghosts?'

Reverend Singh listened disbelievingly to the villager's story.

'And what does the *manush-bagha* look like?' he asked 'Have you seen it?'

'It is like a man in its limbs but with a hideous head—like a ghost, a monster! You have guns and drums with you, Reverend Singh. You can save our village.'

'Perhaps we should build a platform in a tree so we can watch the ghost,' suggested Reverend Singh.

Early next morning, Singh and his companions went out to examine the haunt of the ghosts. They found a giant white-ant mound that was nearly two storeys high. The ants had left, but it seemed the mound had new occupants. The men erected a platform and kept watch. At dusk, three wolves and two cubs appeared at the opening of one of the holes. Close on the heels of the cubs came the 'ghosts', two scrawny figures with thick matted hair. Some of the men levelled their guns to shoot, but Reverend Singh stopped them. The wolves and ghosts disappeared into the jungle.

'They are not ghosts, my friends,' he said, turning to his companions. 'They are children.'

Singh decided the only way to unravel the mystery was to dig out the ant mound, but none of the villagers would go near the haunted place. A couple of days later, Singh managed to persuade some men from another village who hadn't heard the story of the 'ghosts' to help him.

On Sunday 17 October 1920, the men began breaking up the mound with shovels and the wolves came racing out in terror. Only the mother wolf stayed to fight for her territory. She bared her teeth at the intruders and snarled as they approached her with their upraised spades, but the men killed her with bows and arrows. Once she lay dead, work continued quickly. The ant mound was demolished and there, in the centre in a tangle of hair, fur and flesh, two wolf cubs and the two 'ghosts' lay huddled together.

The men threw sheets over their captives and tied them up. They were rewarded with the wolf cubs, which they would be able to sell at the markets for a good price.

Singh took the children. They were girls. He guessed the big girl was around eight years old and the little one was probably still only a toddler of around 18 months, but it was hard to tell. They were filthy, and covered in open sores and scars. Despite being small, they put up a good fight against their captors, scratching and biting anyone who came near them.

Back at the village of Godamuri, Singh built a pen out of poles and placed small bowls of food and water outside the bars. He asked the villagers to take care of the children until he could return with a cart to collect them, and then he went on his way.

Five days later he returned, to find the village abandoned. The two small children had been left in the filth of their cage without food or water. They were so weak from dehydration that Reverend Singh had to tear up his handkerchief, dip it in a cup of tea and when it was soaked, put one end into the mouth of each child in turn. The girls shut their eyes and sucked the liquid from the cloth. When they had recovered some of their strength, Reverend Singh loaded them into a bullock cart and spent a week travelling back to his home at Midnapore.

Taming the wolf children

Reverend Singh and his wife ran an orphanage for abandoned children, so adding two more didn't seem difficult. A few weeks after their arrival, Mrs Singh gave the girls crewcuts. She also named them—the older one Kamala and the younger girl Amala. The girls spent part of their day in a cage in Reverend Singh's office. He was fascinated by them and believed they had been raised by wolves. He kept diaries about the girls and watched them, trying to work out if he could teach them to behave like human beings.

One thing the girls hadn't learnt was how to walk. They got around on all fours most of the time. They liked looting through the rubbish for tasty leftovers and sniffed everything before they ate it. They avoided the other kids and would sit in a corner of the orphanage and stare at the walls for hours on end. For a long time, Mrs Singh couldn't dress them, for the girls would tear the clothes; so she sewed loincloths on to them that they couldn't get out of no matter how they tore at them. At night, the girls slept curled round each other like a pair of puppies.

Although they showed affection for each other, the girls shunned the other children in the orphanage. Benjamin, a toddling baby that tried to befriend them, was bitten and scratched and kept clear of them ever after.

After they had been at the orphanage for several months, Reverend Singh decided it was time they had more freedom. They had been spending most of their time in the cage in his office and when they weren't in the cage they were kept indoors under supervision. In the spring, they were allowed out into the courtyard for a few hours during the day. Someone was always assigned to watch them.

Khiroda was one of the older girls in the orphanage— she'd been found in a bundle of rags on the Singhs' doorstep when she was just a baby. On a sunny Saturday afternoon Khiroda was given the job of watching the wolf-girls. They sat in the shade against the wall and watched the other children playing. Suddenly, Khiroda looked up to see the wolf-girls heading to the garden gate. One of the smaller children had gone out into the garden and left it open. Khiroda ran after them but Amala and Kamala were too fast for her—and too fierce. Khiroda ran screaming back into the orphanage, her arms streaming with blood from the scratches and bites the wild girls had inflicted. The alarm raised, all the orphanage staff went racing after them. Amala and Kamala were found lying quietly in the middle of a thicket of lantana bushes and brought back to the orphanage.

Another cage was built for them in the courtyard underneath a jackfruit tree. The Singhs made sure that if they were not in their cage, a grown-up watched them all the time.

Kamala alone

A year after their arrival at the orphanage, both girls
fell ill. The Singhs hadn't allowed doctors to see the girls
up to now. They were worried that once word spread
about the wolf-children in their care, a stream of curious
visitors would plague them. They also thought no one
would want to marry the girls when they grew up if the
truth about their past became known. But now the girls
were so sick it looked as though they might die. The
Singhs called in a doctor but it was too late for Amala.
She died within days.

Kamala tried to wake her dead sister. She touched her
face, her eyes, her lips. She would not leave the body.
Eventually the Singhs carried her away, and for the next
six days Kamala sat in a corner alone. For weeks she
would go to the places Amala had last been and smell
them, looking for the scent of her companion.

As her grief subsided, Kamala became more attached
to Mrs Singh. She also befriended the animals that lived in
the courtyard and developed a special affection for the
baby goats.

Slowly, over the years, Kamala became used to life in
the orphanage. She began to walk upright and in a small
way learnt to fit in with the humans around her; but
progress was slow. At the end of two years she had learnt
only two words, and she never learnt enough to be able to
explain where she came from.

As the Singhs had feared, a stream of visitors came to
see the so called 'wolf-child'. Kamala, small and wiry in
her thin cotton dress with her head shaved, was brought
out for the guests to stare at.

Nine years after her arrival at the orphanage, Kamala
fell ill and died. She was probably around 17 years old.

Lost children

The Singhs reckoned that Amala and Kamala had been raised by wolves, but people who really know about the lives of wolves find it pretty hard to believe that they would bother to raise human babies. They're usually busy enough looking after their own cubs without having to worry about a scrawny furless fuzzball. Like Victor, Amala and Kamala were probably abandoned because they had problems that their families couldn't cope with—maybe they were mentally disabled.

The kid in the next story was neglected and abandoned too, but not in the wild. His story is really strange, even for a feral kid; in fact, it's one of the great unsolved puzzles of history.

The mysterious boy

Nuremberg, Germany, 28 May 1828
It was late afternoon and long shadows stretched across the cobbled street. A boy lurched from one side of the street to the other, leaning on the wall to help support himself. A man was watching him.

'Are you lost, boy?' asked the man.

The boy stared at him blankly.

'Do you need some directions? I've been watching you this past half hour and you're walking around in circles. Where are you heading to? Where do you want to go?'

The man used hand gestures to indicate directions because he could see the boy was struggling to understand him, although he looked to be somewhere between 14 and 16 years of age.

'The tower,' replied the boy.

'The tower? Now what tower would that be, then?'

The boy sighed and swayed unsteadily on his feet. The man noticed the letter he was clutching and asked who it was for. There was no answer, so the man gently took it from him. It was addressed to 'The Captain of the Light Horse in Nuremberg, near the New Gate'.

'Ah, it's the New Gate you're after, I can take you there.'

The boy stared at him with sad eyes and said, 'I want to be a rider like my father.'

No one at the captain's house knew what to make of the strange boy. They offered him meat and a mug of beer, but he spat the food out in disgust. When he was offered bread and water, he ate and drank with relief. He could only answer their questions by saying 'Dunno,' and 'I want to be a rider like my father.'

As the captain was away, the strange boy was shown out to the stable, where he immediately fell asleep in the hay. He seemed exhausted. When the captain returned he was as mystified as his servants had been. He took the strange visitor to the police station, where the boy answered all questions with the same two replies.

'I want to be such a one as my father was,' he wept.

He had two letters in his possession, neither of which did much to explain who he was or how he came to be in Nuremberg. They raised more questions than they answered. The police decided to give him a name—Kaspar Hauser.

The child of Nuremberg

News of the strange boy being kept at the police station quickly spread through Nuremberg, and all kinds of people came to visit him. They found a teenager 140 cm tall with soft down on his lips, pale blue eyes and soft curly brown hair. Except for the strange expression he so often wore, he had an attractive face. He had arrived in Nuremberg in a strange collection of mismatched clothes: a round felt hat lined with yellow silk and stitched with red leather, a black silk scarf, a grey cloth jacket, a linen vest with red dots and a pair of riding pants. His toes stuck out through the ends of his boots. In his pocket was a white and red checked handkerchief with a 'K' embroidered on it, and a small envelope with some gold dust inside.

Every visitor tried to engage Kaspar in conversation, but he found company tiring and his expression would quickly become glazed if anyone asked too many questions. He had such a small collection of words that his jailer couldn't help but notice how often he said the word 'horse'. Because of this, one of the policemen had the bright idea of giving him a wooden horse. Kaspar was ecstatic and wept with happiness when he was handed the toy. Soon he had built up a collection of wooden horses that his visitors brought him and he spent much of his day in prison decorating them and pretending to feed them.

Andreas Hiltel, the jailer at the Nuremberg tower, supplied him with paper and crayons. When Kaspar wasn't tending his horses he drew, until every wall of his cell was covered with pictures from floor to ceiling.

Hiltel brought his children to play with Kaspar. Kaspar liked 11-year-old Julius immediately but he found two-year-old Margaret too scary. She was so small and loud that Kaspar looked alarmed whenever she entered his cell.

'Margaret—she hurt Kaspar?' he asked. Julius laughed

and reassured him that Margaret was harmless, even if she was annoying.

The boys struck up a friendship and Julius took it on himself to teach Kaspar how to speak. Unlike Victor and the wolf-girls, Kaspar was a fast learner. Every day Julius helped Kaspar expand his vocabulary until Kaspar could communicate with his visitors in a basic way.

'Kaspar many visitors today, Julius,' said Kaspar. 'Kaspar like the lady with the tail.'

'A tail?' asked Julius

'She come with the man with the mountain.' said Kaspar seriously.

Julius looked at his father and raised his eyebrows.

'I think he's talking about a lady with a long shawl that dragged along the ground,' said Herr Hiltel. 'She came with a big fat fellow—that must be the man with the mountain.'

So late in the world

After several months in the jail, Kaspar was moved to the house of a local teacher, Professor Daumer. No one had been able to find out anything more about where Kaspar had come from, and he still couldn't explain it himself. His fame had spread from Nuremberg to all of Germany. Newspaper articles began to appear about him across Europe. Though the people of Nuremberg had called him their child, he soon became known as 'the child of Europe'. His sweet nature and innocent manner charmed nearly everyone who met him.

Kaspar could give almost no explanation about where he had come from. It seemed he had been kept in secret isolation for the whole of his childhood. The strange letters he had carried, the packet of gold dust and the strange old-fashioned clothes he had been found in added to the mystery. In some ways, he was like a new-born baby—he knew so little about the world.

Professor Daumer set about teaching Kaspar how to read and write. Kaspar learnt quickly, and never tired of asking questions. There was so much to find out.

'I am already so old and still have to learn what children have already known for so long,' he said. 'Sometimes I wish I had never come out of my cage. I have come into the world so late...'

One August night, as he stood at his bedroom window he called out to the professor.

'Who put the candles in the sky, professor?' he asked. 'I have never seen the night sky before. It is so beautiful.'

Kaspar believed everything in the world had a life and understanding like his own. He found it confusing to have to distinguish between the feelings of animals and people. He had long and interesting conversations with the professor's cat.

'I have seen your cousin, Herr Cat. Doesn't that interest you?' asked Kaspar as he stroked the cat on the windowsill. 'Your cousin, I'm sure it was your cousin—he looked just like you so he must be your relative. Also, today I saw a dog, very well behaved, Herr Cat. He had such nice manners. I am sure if you tried you could be like him.'

Unravelling the past

Gradually Kaspar became capable of talking about his past, but it all sounded like a strange dream. As Kaspar often couldn't distinguish between what he dreamt and reality, it was even harder to make sense of his story. He said that he had been kept in a cellar that was only two metres by one metre, with two tiny windows set in its ceiling. There was nothing in the cellar but straw, two wooden horses and a wooden dog. For as long as he could remember, he had lived in this prison. All he could do was sleep, eat and decorate his toy horses with a collection of red ribbons. When he woke, a small piece of fresh bread would be there for him, and some water in a jug.

Towards the end of his time in the cellar, a man had come to him and tried to teach him how to write his name. For weeks on end the man tried to teach Kaspar how to pray as well, and when Kaspar failed to understand he was beaten.

One day, the man lifted Kaspar up and carried him out of the cellar. Kaspar fainted with the pain of having to stretch his legs after years spent on his hands and knees. The man spent several days teaching Kaspar how to walk, but the boy's knees were permanently damaged from years of inactivity. Every step was painful. The man promised him he would have his own horse if he co-operated. Eventually the mysterious stranger abandoned him in Nuremberg with the letters.

The man in black

Eighteen months after Kaspar arrived in Nuremberg, an incident occurred that showed his past was more tangled and mysterious than anyone had imagined.

Kaspar was in the outside toilet when he saw a man's feet at the door. He was too afraid to move. He sensed that something was wrong. Kaspar had always been afraid of black—black horses and black hens both frightened him. When Kaspar went back into the house, he heard footsteps. The man—clothed completely in black with his face masked by a black handkerchief—was in the hallway.

He lunged at Kaspar with a knife and Kaspar fell to the ground, unconscious. When he came to, he was covered in blood. Terrified that the man would return to finish him off, he staggered into the basement where he blacked out.

Hours later, Professor Daumer's mother discovered Kaspar in the basement, lying in a pool of blood with a long deep gash across his forehead.

An English lord who had taken an interest in Kaspar's case decided it was no longer safe for Kaspar to stay in Nuremberg. He organised for Kaspar to live with a different teacher 80 km away in the city of Ansbach. The new teacher, Meyer, was a cruel man who had little sympathy for Kaspar's gentle ways. Kaspar began to feel he was in prison again.

Two years later, a strange man lured Kaspar into the court garden in the Orangerie. He told Kaspar he had a message from his mother and promised it would reveal who Kaspar really was. When they were alone, the stranger stabbed Kaspar in the chest with a dagger and left him for dead. Kaspar struggled back to the house of his teacher.

At first Meyer refused to believe Kaspar, and forced him to walk back to the Orangerie to show where the attack had happened. Finally, when Kaspar revealed his wound, he was put to bed, delirious with pain.

'Many cats are the death of the mouse,' said Kaspar. 'Tired, very tired, still have to take a long trip.'

He died three days later on 14 December 1833.

The lost prince?

Kaspar was probably no more than 21 years old when he was murdered. Many people believe he was the lost Prince of Baden, who was kidnapped from his cradle because his relatives wanted to inherit his kingdom, but the mystery of his origins has never been properly solved.

In 1924 at the castle of Schloss Pilsach near Nuremberg, workmen who were renovating the building found a tiny dungeon. Inside, amongst the debris, was a little white wooden horse.

Whoever he was, Kaspar Hauser, the child of Europe, has haunted the imagination of the world ever since he appeared on the streets of Nuremberg.

4 SUPERSTARS

FAME, FORTUNE AND
HITTING THE BIG TIME

I reckon
I could be famous
if I could just
think up something
that I'd want to be
famous for. I've got
a bit of a gift for
making spitballs but
that's about it.

I used to like the idea of being famous—
Milo the Megastar. I reckon it'd be cool to have a big
fan club. But after I'd collected a bunch of stories
about famous kids, I started to change my mind.
I like mooching around too much to work that hard.

The kid who knew what he wanted

Yehudi leant forward in his seat and tilted his blond head
to one side so he could hear better. He was sitting with
his parents in a theatre listening to the San Francisco
Symphony Orchestra perform with a violinist called

Louis Persinger. It was a regular Saturday event for the Menuhin family, and Yehudi loved it—sitting high up in the darkened gallery. He closed his eyes and imagined he was flying with the music.

Afterwards, Yehudi asked the same question he asked after every concert.

'Could I have a violin, please Mama, please Papa.'

'One day, Yehudi,' replied his mother.

Yehudi's parents were having trouble finding enough money to pay the rent and besides, Yehudi was only three years old. There was plenty of time, if only he would be patient. But Yehudi couldn't wait.

The tin fiddle

All of the Menuhins' friends and relations heard about Yehudi's plea. For his fourth birthday, a friend of the family went to Macy's department store and bought him a smart toy violin. It was made from tin and was just the right size for a four-year-old. Yehudi would be able to pretend he was a great concert violinist, just like Louis Persinger.

Yehudi could hardly contain his excitement as he peeled back the wrapping paper of his birthday present and saw what lay inside—the longed-for violin. He lifted it from the box and laughed with pleasure. At last! The grown-ups all smiled as he tucked the instrument beneath his chin and closed his eyes to concentrate. He raised the toy bow and drew it across the strings, to produce a rough squeaky noise.

Yehudi's face distorted with rage. He threw the tin violin and the bow on the ground and sobbed.

'It doesn't sing!' he shouted. 'I hate it! I want a real violin! I want a violin that sings!'

A few months later, when Yehudi's grandmother heard the story about the birthday present, she sent some money to cover the cost of a real wooden violin for her grandson. It took some time to persuade Louis Persinger to take Yehudi on as his pupil. Yehudi was taught by someone else to begin with, but once Persinger heard the boy play, he knew there was something special about him.

Practising perfection

Yehudi Menuhin was born in New York City on 22 April 1916. His family moved to California in 1918.

By the time Yehudi was seven, he was ready for his first public performance. Persinger accompanied him on the piano at a recital by the San Francisco Orchestra. The boy caused a sensation, and word of his incredible ability began to spread across America.

It was obvious to Yehudi's parents that he was a different kind of kid. They sent him to school for one day before deciding he was better off learning at home with his two little sisters, Hephzibah and Yaltah. His mother taught the children to read and write, and Yehudi happily spent three hours a day practising his violin.

As Yehudi's reputation spread, people invited him to travel to Europe and study under some of the most famous musicians in the world.

When he was 10, Yehudi was invited to perform at Carnegie Hall with the New York Symphony Orchestra. Only the best performers in the world got to play at Carnegie Hall, and orchestra members couldn't believe the chubby blond kid would be up to it. The conductor suggested to Yehudi that he should play a simple piece by Mozart, but Yehudi insisted on doing a really difficult Beethoven concerto.

When Yehudi had to ask the conductor to tune his violin because the pegs were too hard for him to turn, the other musicians were even more suspicious. They all grumbled to themselves. How could this little squirt possibly lead the whole orchestra in such a difficult piece of music!

Triumph and tours

On 27 November 1927, Yehudi stepped out onto the stage at Carnegie Hall and into history. The audience and the orchestra were bowled over by his playing, and plans were set in motion for his first nationwide tour.

Yehudi owned two quite reasonable violins, but he had to borrow a top-quality instrument for his concerts. When one of his rich fans heard that Yehudi performed on borrowed instruments, he invited the Menuhins to visit him.

'You must choose any violin you want,' announced the millionaire. 'No matter what the price. Choose it; it's yours.'

Yehudi picked a violin with a sweet and mellow sound. It was named 'Prince Khevenhüller' and had been made by the famous Italian violin-maker Stradivarius in the eighteenth century. Stradivarius violins are worth millions of dollars each.

Yehudi was so successful that his father decided to give up his job as a teacher so he could manage Yehudi's career. Together they toured America and the world for several months of each year. By the time he was 17, Yehudi had performed all over Europe, America and Australia. He made recordings and commissioned new music from composers. Many pieces were written especially for him.

When Yehudi grew up, he married twice and had four kids, one of whom became a pianist. As well as continuing to play violin, Yehudi began to conduct orchestras. His energy and interest in everything around him made him one of the most sought-after musicians in the world. He performed to audiences in every corner of the world from South America to India. He learnt to play jazz and Indian music, wrote books and became involved in countless organisations that fight for peace and human rights. He even took up yoga; he believed that headstands helped his playing.

In 1963 he opened a music school in London, and in 1965 Queen Elizabeth made him a knight, and then later a lord. He is only the second musician in history to receive this honour. He finally took his title—Lord Menuhin of Stoke D'Abernon—in 1985, when he became a British citizen. Right up to the very end of his life, he toured the world, conducting concerts and sharing the joy he found in music. He died on 12 March 1999, aged 82, while visiting Berlin—a legend in his own lifetime.

The Kalgoorlie kid

Yehudi Menuhin was really gifted, but he also had a lot of lucky breaks. He had the opportunity to study with top teachers from an early age, and his mum and dad made sure he had plenty of help. This next story is about a kid who had to fight to get herself noticed—a girl with a gift and a lot of grit who shook the dust of the Western Australian goldfields from her shoes and headed out into the world to become an international star.

Going for gold

Eileen stood in front of the shop window and pressed her face against the glass until a small foggy cloud appeared.

'What is that, Mum?' she asked, staring at the huge, dark, shiny instrument in the music-shop window.

'Surely you know it's a piano, Eileen.'

'It looks so grand—it must make a big sound. How does it work? '

'You see those white things and the little black ones—they're the keys and you push them down to make the music.'

'It must be so much nicer than a mouth organ. I'd do anything to have one.'

'One day I'll show you how it works. One day when Daddy's struck gold and we're rich we'll have one, and then you can play all you like, my darling.'

It was 1919 and Eileen and her mum were in Melbourne on their way to the West Australian goldfields. Eileen was seven years old and until then, she and her mother had lived in Zeehan, Tasmania, in a little hut at the foot of a mountain.

After years in the west searching for gold, her dad had written to tell them he had enough to pay their fares. From Melbourne, they took a steamship to Adelaide and a wagon across the Nullarbor Plain. Eileen made herself a mattress from straw and sacking and slept by the campfire on the long journey west to Kununoppin, a tent city on the edge of the goldfields.

The pub piano

Life was tough for the Joyces, and in two years her father's lucky seam had petered out. The family had to move on again. In 1921 they settled in Kalgoorlie and Eileen's father took up work in someone else's mine. Her mother took in laundry and Eileen was sent to a Catholic convent school. The richer girls at the school were taught piano by one of the nuns and Eileen longed to have lessons too, but they cost sixpence each and the Joyces never had a penny to spare.

One day her mother took her down to the local pub. At the back of the bar room stood a battered and beer-stained upright piano. It was out of tune and some of the keys didn't work at all, but Eileen's mum taught her how to play the popular tunes that they both knew and every afternoon, Eileen would slip into the cool dark pub and tinkle the keys.

Eileen had a fiery temper and a fierce determination. She took to busking in the streets of Kalgoorlie. After school, she would walk to the edge of town where the miners were returning from work and play her mouth organ. She made sure her father never caught her, and she kept her pennies in a tin in the little lean-to that she slept in at the back of the family bungalow. When a neighbouring boy stole her hard-won savings, she punched his lights out. She was going to have piano lessons and nothing was going to stop her.

Birthday present

At the beginning of the new term, Eileen approached the nun who taught piano and held out her sixpence.

Eileen was the fastest-learning pupil that the convent had ever seen. Word spread of her ability and a generous stranger paid for her lessons to continue.

On the night of her 10th birthday, Eileen climbed the steps to the pub and hurried into the bar room for a quick practice session before going home for her birthday tea. To her horror, there was an empty space where the piano had been.

Eileen walked home in a state of misery. She tried to look enthusiastic about the party tea that her mother spread out on the kitchen table.

'By the way, Eileen,' said her mother, 'there's a little something for you in your room.'

Eileen opened the door to her bedroom and stared. Her uncle and father laughed at her expression as they stood on either side of the pub piano. When Eileen lifted the lid and touched the keys she found the piano had been tuned and all the damaged keys repaired. She threw her arms around her father and hugged him tight.

Perth and Percy

Everyone in Kalgoorlie came to know of the extraordinary kid at the convent school who could play the piano like a virtuoso. The local priest wrote to the best Catholic school in Perth, Loreto Convent, and asked them to take Eileen as a scholarship student.

So at 12 years of age, Eileen kissed her parents goodbye and headed off to boarding school and a whole new world of possibilities. Not long after she arrived at the school the famous composer, Percy Grainger, and an international pianist, William Backhaus, came to visit Loreto. Friends had told them of the gifted young prodigy, and they wanted to see her for themselves. They were so impressed that they wrote letters to the newspaper asking the people of Perth to help Eileen study in America or Europe.

Back in Kalgoorlie, the miners got together to help pay Eileen's expenses. None of them had forgotten the fiery kid that had stood busking on street corners, and everyone wanted to help. When a couple of rich Perth businessmen offered to chip in as well, the public fund to help Eileen Joyce was up and running.

Leipzig, London and the world

In September 1927, before her 15th birthday, Eileen enrolled at the Leipzig Conservatorium of Music, where gifted performers from all over the world came to study under some of the best teachers in Europe. By the time she was 18, she was being invited to perform as soloist with some of the world's top philharmonic orchestras. The miners of Kalgoorlie followed her successes in the newspapers as she went on to perform for the BBC and record the soundtracks for British movies. Eileen came home to tour Australia twice during the 1930s. During World War II, she toured the bombed cities and towns of Europe with the London Philharmonic Orchestra in an effort to raise people's spirits, even though her own husband had been killed in wartime action with the Royal Navy.

In 1950, a film was made of Eileen's life which documented her journey from the goldfields of Western Australia to the concert halls of Europe. Eileen spent most of her life touring the world from South Africa to the Soviet Union—she became Australia's most travelled musician. Her career as a concert pianist continued until 1962, when she retired from public performing.

Hollywood heroine

At the same time as little Yehudi Menuhin was wowing world audiences with his violin playing, a chubby-cheeked three-year-old named Shirley Temple started up dance lessons at Mrs Meglin's Dance Studio in Los Angeles, California. She spent two years hoofing around with a bunch of other pre-school kids before she was 'discovered'. One day in 1932, a pair of movie-makers turned up at the dance studio looking for kids to star in a series of short films they were making. Shirley didn't like the look of them. She hid under the piano and cringed when one of the men pointed to her and said, 'We want that one.'

The black box

Shirley made six short films for the Educational Film Corporation, but the only thing educational about them was what Shirley learnt about work.

'This isn't playtime, kids,' said the director on the first day of filming. 'It's work.'

One other little girl and a whole tribe of boys performed in the films with Shirley. The films were called 'Baby Burlesks' and featured a bunch of kids pretending to be grown-ups. Shirley discovered acting could be pretty dangerous. She was tied to a stake and pelted with clods of mud, knocked flat in a wrestle with a boy, and seated in a cart which was tied to a frantic ostrich that zigzagged across the sound stage before colliding with a wall, throwing Shirley from the cart.

The children's mothers weren't allowed onto the set, and any kids that misbehaved were punished by being put inside a black box, with a block of ice inside it. You could stand, you could lie down in the puddle or you could sit on the ice block in the total darkness. After two sessions in the black box, Shirley paid close attention to what was asked of her.

By the end of 1933, five-year-old Shirley had made

eight Baby Burlesks, appeared in five comedy shorts, had six 'walk-on' parts and one bit part in a bigger movie.

Then Shirley was cast as the lead in a movie called *Little Miss Marker*. It made her a star. There were a lot of child stars before her and there have been many since, but none that have made as big an impact on the world.

Mud pies, mud pies

Shirley Jane Temple was born 23 April 1928. She had dimples, heaps of curly blond hair and loads of spunk. In most ways she was just an ordinary kid who wanted to do ordinary kid things; but even simple things can get complicated when you're a superstar.

Shirley had a bodyguard to protect her from kidnapping, and he had to follow her everywhere she went. Her home was surrounded by a two-metre chain link fence. A photo-electric eye guarded her bedroom window, and every other window in the house was fitted with electric circuit sensors connected to the local police headquarters. But Shirley could still find ways to get into trouble.

Shirley lived in Hollywood, and all day every day, busloads of tourists stopped outside to gawk at the home of the biggest star of 1934. A tour driver would recite everything he knew about her family. Sometimes Shirley would watch, squatting in the bushes behind the fence. Even though she generated millions of dollars for the movie studio that she worked for, she got very little pocket money of her own, and like any kid, she was always scheming to increase her piggybank savings. One day, as she sat in the bushes watching the tourists get off the morning bus, she had a brainwave.

Building work was being done on her house and Shirley struck a deal with the builders. Next morning, when the first tourist bus arrived, she was ready, standing outside the gate. Her bodyguard stood beside her, watching with a disapproving frown. In front of her was a neat row of mud pies lined up along the pavement. She'd made a little sign that they were for sale—small ones 5 cents, large 25 cents. They sold out instantly. The bus drivers were enthusiastic and Shirley was kept busy squashing more goop into her mother's pie tins.

The bodyguard became uneasy about the crowds of strangers and went and 'dobbed' Shirley in to her mother. Mrs Temple quickly came running down to the gate.

'No more mud pies.' she said disapprovingly.

'They aren't mud,' Shirley replied. 'They're cement.'

Mud or no mud, Shirley was given a lecture about talking to strangers and marched back up to the house, but not before she'd pocketed her earnings.

Million-dollar baby

Shirley never tired of performing. She had a huge amount of energy and could outstrip most adults—especially when it came to dancing for hours on end.

There was no time for school. Shirley had her own private tutor, who gave her lessons in between film takes in her own private bungalow on the movie lot.

Celebrities from all around the world came to visit her. Everyone wanted to know her, including all the other famous movie stars in Hollywood as well as presidents and princes. By the time she was six, Shirley was one of the most famous faces in the world. Millions of dolls were made in her image—every little girl wanted a 'Shirley Temple' doll of their own.

For her eighth birthday in 1936, Shirley was sent over 135 000 presents from all around the world, including a pair of wallabies. Of course Shirley couldn't keep so much stuff, and most of it was given to charity. Her parents did let her keep the white model racing car with red leather seats that had its own lawnmower engine, but when Shirley bumped into someone on her first spin around the studio grounds, the car was relegated to the garage at home.

Getting down to business

Between the ages of six and 14, Shirley starred in 24 films. She cheered up America and a world caught in poverty and depression, and her films earned enough money to rescue the movie company Twentieth Century Fox from big debt. She made millions of dollars for the people who were connected with her career.

You'd think that Shirley would have been rich, but through a combination of bad luck and bad management there was very little left of her fortune by the time she'd grown up. Shirley gave up acting when she was in her twenties, and after having three kids, got interested in politics instead.

Not all kid superstars have been half as lucky (or half as famous). Performing is really hard work and not every child loves it as much as Shirley Temple did. Most child stars have a pretty rough time. Shirley Temple and Yehudi Menuhin both had very protective parents that managed to shield them from the downside of being a star. But plenty of kids wind up being forced to work really long days and get caught up in a world of grown-up problems from drug addiction to bankruptcy. There are hundreds of

child stars whose adult lives are a big downhill slide.
Many of them have ended up suing their parents for
the money that they worked so hard to earn. Some,
like Macaulay Culkin of the 'Home Alone' movies, even
resort to 'divorcing' one or both of their parents in the
course of court battles about where all the money
has gone.

Child stars can generate millions of dollars of income
in a very short period of time, but often their fame is
shortlived and they're quickly forgotten. If you really
want to be remembered, setting world sporting records
is a better place to start.

Shane Gould, golden girl

Shane looked up. There they were again—those signs.
'All that glitters is not Gould.' A grinning American was
waving it as he stood in the stands overlooking the
Munich Olympic pool. Shane nodded shyly and walked
on by.

Shane felt excited and confident as she readied herself
for the 400-metre freestyle. She knew she was ready for
this race and she knew she could win it. Swimming was
Shane's life. Ever since she was nine years old and had
won her first silver medal at the New South Wales
Swimming Championship, she'd been working towards
Olympic gold.

When the starting gun went off, Shane cut the water
like a knife. She knew she was swimming well—she felt
light and smooth. The water seemed to rush past beneath
her. All her movements were precise, her arm strokes
exact and powerful. The other competitors didn't have a
chance. She took the lead and held it for the entire race.

When Shane climbed out of the pool and mounted the podium to receive her gold medal she became the youngest Australian Olympic medallist in history. She was 15 years old.

Water baby

Shane Elizabeth Gould was born in Sydney on 23 November 1956. She loved the water from babyhood. When bathtime was over, she cried to get back in the water. Before she was three she could swim underwater at the pool with her eyes open, and at five she was snorkelling around the reefs of Fiji. By the time she was 15 years old, she held every women's world freestyle record from 100 m to 1500 m.

Shane had the perfect physique for a swimmer—tall and slim with wide shoulders and narrow hips. By the time she was 13 she knew that her gift for swimming was something special—she gave up all other interests and gave herself over to competitive swimming. She set her alarm for early-morning training, watched her diet and kept a logbook of her training routines. Her persistence and single-mindedness paid off. Between April 1971 and January 1972, she set seven new world records. By July of 1972, she was so confident that she'd win gold at the Games that she asked her parents if she could have her braces removed just for the competition. She knew the cameras would be flashing and she wanted to look her best.

Shane Gould won three gold, one silver and a bronze medal at the 1972 Olympics. She is the only Australian in history to have won five medals at a single Olympics. In the same year she was voted both ABC Sportsman of the Year and Australian of the Year.

When the race is over

Australia and the swimming world were amazed when
Shane decided to retire from competitive swimming in
1973. Her coach tried to change her mind, but Shane's
mum and dad had always told her to give up swimming if
it stopped being fun. Shane had achieved more than many
athletes achieve in a lifetime and she was tired of being in
the spotlight. Three years later, at 19, she married Neil
Innes and they set up a farm in Western Australia and
started a family. Her new passions were her four children
and the life she shared with Neil. In 1981, Shane was
awarded an MBE (member of the Order of the British
Empire). 'I deserve it more for being a mother than for
winning races,' she said to the press. Shane eventually
worked as a consultant to retiring sportspeople to help
them make the shift from competitive sport to the
ordinary world. Stepping out of the limelight and making
a new life for yourself can take a lot of guts.

A passion for pictures

Alexandra felt all floppy. She lay on the sofa in the living
room and picked at a loose thread on one of the cushions.
Her mum looked in around the door and frowned at the
sight of her miserable four-year-old daughter.

'Alexandra, why don't you go outside and play? It's
such a nice sunny day out there—why do you have to lie
there and sulk?'

'I want my colouring books back,' said Alexandra,
pushing her blonde hair out of her eyes and glaring
at her mother.

'Alexandra, I told you before, I'm not buying

any more colouring books for you. You spend too much time with them. You need to learn to do other things too.'

'I want my crayons,' she shouted.

'Go out and play, darling,' replied her mother.

'I don't want to play, Mama. I want to draw.'

Drawing like breathing

Not being able to draw was like not being able to breathe for Alexandra Nechita. Even though her mum and dad stopped buying her colouring books, Alexandra wasn't going to give up her passion. When she finally got the crayons back, she took to drawing her own pictures on the back of computer paper that her mum brought home from work.

Alexandra Nechita was destined to be the first painting prodigy in history. She was born in Romania on 27 August 1985, but when she was one year old her parents immigrated to America. They settled in a little bungalow in Los Angeles.

When Alexandra was two, her parents bought her first set of crayons. By the time she was five, she was using watercolour paints. Alexandra could draw and paint for hours without stopping. At seven, she moved on to painting in oils and acrylics on real canvas. Her parents bought her what she needed but sometimes they wished she wouldn't use quite as much colour in the lively pictures she produced—she was costing them a fortune in materials. They set aside a little area for her to use as a studio, but the bungalow began to fill up with her work.

When she was eight, they enrolled her in art classes; but after looking at her work, the teacher realised Alexandra had a unique talent that she was better off developing by herself, and sent her home again.

The bungalow was getting so crowded that her parents decided to exhibit Alexandra's work in local libraries, and soon sold her first picture for $50.

Eventually, an artist's agent spotted one of her paintings and was impressed. When he was told that the painter was only eight years old, he thought it was a hoax and refused to believe it. He tracked down the Nechita family and asked if he could watch Alexandra at work. After watching her paint for a couple of hours he realised Alexandra's gift was both genuine and unique. He decided to promote the young prodigy.

On 1 April 1994—the day she became an American citizen—Alexandra had her first commercial exhibition. She was still only eight years old.

Pint-sized Picasso

By the time she was 11, Alexandra had earned more than $5 million from the sale of her art work. She was dubbed a 'Pint-sized Picasso' by some of her fans, and art collectors around the world competed to buy up her work. Some of her paintings now sell for more than $100 000!

Alexandra has produced hundreds of paintings, and her work is in demand all over the world. She reckons she'd still spend all her time painting, even if people only paid her $1 for what she does. She does it because she loves to paint—she *has* to paint. That's what being a superstar means—absolute dedication to what you do.

5 BATTLERS

BREAKING THE CHAINS

Kids who are superstars are hard workers—you have to be to make it to the top; but at least superstars get rewarded for all their hard slog. For most working kids, life's a real battle. Working because you have to just to survive is pretty different to working simply because you want to. Working kids have to be really tough because they get stuck with some of the toughest stuff around.

Put through the mill

Lancashire, England, 1799

'Robert, Robert, did you hear the news?' said little Mary Richards as she slid into place at the workhouse dinner table. 'The owner of the great cotton mill in Nottingham, Lamberts—he's offered work to all us children. He's going to turn us into ladies and gents. There will be roast beef and plum pudding and we'll have silver watches and the like. The master—he'll even let us ride his horses. An' there'll be plenty of cash to line our pockets with too!'

'Well, I s'pose it'd be better than working as a sweep,'

said Robert. He was seven, the same age as Mary but he'd already had some experience of the world outside the workhouse. The year before, when he was still only six, he'd been sent out to clean chimneys.

'Aye, that was terrible work for you, wasn't it?' said Mary.

'Mmmm, I just couldn't get up the chimneys fast enough. The master—he'd light matches and burn the bottom of my feet trying to hurry me up. Problem was, I was too scared of all that blackness. After I got stuck in one chimney and was too afrightened to go up or come down, he sent me back, saying I'd never make a sweep.'

Robert Blincoe couldn't even remember his parents. He and Mary Richards had both lived in St Pancras Workhouse since they were tiny, along with other orphans and homeless poor people who worked there to pay for their keep.

In 1799, a local cotton mill (a factory where raw cotton was spun and turned into cloth) approached the workhouse and struck a deal with the wardens to take over the children until they were 21. On a sunny summer day, 80 boys and girls aged seven years were loaded into carts that lined up outside the workhouse.

Slop and black bread

When they reached the mill, they were herded into a big commonroom with long narrow tables and wooden benches. Robert and Mary were separated, she to sit with the girls and he with the boys. There was no cloth, no plates, no knives or forks. Robert pushed away his feelings of unease and concentrated on the exciting thought of plum pudding. He'd never eaten it before, but the idea made his mouth water.

A woman came in with a big black pot and tipped a ladle of thin blue slop into the bowls. Each child was given a piece of black bread to have with the slop.

Robert looked down at his bowl in disgust.

'I can't eat it,' said the boy next to him, 'though I'm right starving.'

The bread was bitter, and so soft that the black dough stuck to their teeth and made the boys look as if all their teeth had been knocked out. Robert gagged as he forced himself to swallow.

There was a clatter at the door as the apprentices from the mill arrived, girls and boys. They were a thin and scruffy gang, their hair stood on end and they were bare-foot. When the overseer nodded, they rushed to a hatch door and jostled each other as a woman opened it. The boys pulled their shirts out and the girls held up their greasy aprons to catch some hot potatoes that she doled out.

'Why, they're like animals!' exclaimed Robert to the boy next to him.

The apprentices wolfed down their potato and then, seeing the new kids, crowded around their table like a band of ragged starlings.

'Here, out of the way,' said a big boy, as he elbowed Robert to one side.

He grabbed Robert's bowl and licked the last drops of porridge from the bottom before snatching up the crusts of the horrid black bread and cramming them into his mouth. Robert watched him with disgust. Little did he know that within a few weeks he would look and behave exactly like this boy.

The boys were shown up two flights of dark winding stairs to their bedrooms. Robert was paired up with the big hungry boy who'd elbowed him at supper. None of the new children were allowed to share with their friends. The bigger boy couldn't wait to get into bed and fell asleep instantly. The stench of oily clothes and the boy's blackened greasy skin turned Robert's stomach. He curled into a little ball with his back to the other boy and cried himself to sleep.

The working day

The next day Robert was sent to work at 5.30 in the morning. The air in the millhouse was thick with dust and his throat and eyes began to sting. All around him, huge machines whirled and roared.

'Well, boy, I'm Mr Smith,' said the overlooker who organised the workers, 'and your job is to collect all the loose cotton that's fallen to the floor.'

After three hours of stooping and gathering, Robert's back began to ache. The stench from the machines and the little fragments of cotton in the air were making him feel sick. He sat down on the floor to rest for a moment.

'Oi, boy, what do you think you're doing?' shouted Mr Smith, cuffing him across the back of his head. 'I won't have any slackers in this mill. Get up and get back to work.'

At twelve o'clock—after six and a half hours of stooping and gathering—a bell rang somewhere in the cotton mill and the master indicated Robert could stop. He knelt down on the floor with relief.

The work Robert was doing was called scavenging and was actually very dangerous. He would often have to wriggle under the machines on his stomach and sometimes tufts of his hair would be caught and torn out by the whirring machinery. Accidents were especially likely when he was tired. Sometimes the children would be so exhausted from working for over 15 hours a day that they grew drowsy. Then the overlooker would pick them up by the ankles and dip them in a big barrel of cold water that stood in a corner of the room to force them awake.

For shame

After a few months of scavenging, Robert was promoted to being a winder. He was still so little that they had to place him on a block so he could reach his work. He worked as quickly as he could, but he couldn't wind the cotton on fast enough. Mr Smith took to him with a stick and beat him till blood gushed from his nose and mouth. Robert shrieked and raised his arms to protect his head, but the blows kept falling.

'Sir, sir, I'm trying, I'm working as fast as I can,' he wept.

Downstairs, on the ground floor of the cotton mill, a blacksmith named William Palfrey was hammering at his forge when he felt something dripping from the ceiling. He slid his hand across the back of his neck and his palm was red with blood.

'Not again,' he muttered and reached for a crowbar.

He leapt up onto a bench and pounded at the ceiling.

'For shame! For shame! Are you murdering the children?' roared the blacksmith 'I'll not stand for it, you animals! Stop it up there, or I'll come up and stop you myself!'

Mr Smith stopped the flogging.

'Thank God for William Palfrey,' said one of the other apprentices to Robert as he helped him to his feet. 'If it weren't for him, we'd be beaten even worse. But he goes home to Litton at seven o'clock, and there's no mercy for us then.'

Blood and cotton

The boys and girls were kept completely separate at the
mills, not like at the workhouse where they had often
played together. Robert would wave to Mary sometimes
at lunchtime, but if he tried to talk to her he got a cuffing.
Robert thought she was still the prettiest girl in the place,
no matter how thin she had grown.

They had been at the workhouse for nearly three years
when the accident happened. Mary worked at a machine
which drew the cotton out ready for spinning. Clumpy
wads of cotton were stretched across a series of frames
that moved past her, and Mary's small hands would fly
across the moving frames, pushing the loose cotton into
place. Underneath the machine was a shaft by which the
frames were turned. One evening, Mary's ripped and tatty
apron caught in the machinery and drew her with it. Her
shrieks rose up above the whirr of the machines.

'Mary!' screamed Robert as he stopped his loom and
leapt down from his box. He felt he was running in slow
motion as he pushed past the overlooker.

'Mary, Mary,' he cried in agony as he stood helplessly
watching his friend whirled round and round in the shaft.
It only took a moment but it seemed to last forever. Blood
streamed across the floor as Mary was drawn tighter into
the works of the machine. He covered his ears to block
out the sound of her bones snapping, her screams and
then the terrible silence as the blood spattered across the
frame and the cotton turned red.

'Help her, stop the machinery! Oh God, stop the
machinery!' he sobbed but the machines stopped of their
own accord as Mary lay jammed between the shafts and
the floor.

For once, everything was quiet in the room. Robert

covered his face with his hands as they extracted the little girl from beneath the shaft. Every bone was broken, her head crushed, her body lifeless.

Mary was not quite 10 years old.

After the mills

Robert finished his apprenticeship in 1813, and four years later he left the mill and set up a small cotton-spinning business. He was physically small, and crippled by his experiences in the cotton mills—his hands were gnarled and his knees deformed from the long hours of standing at the loom. Despite bad luck with fire, debt and other misfortune, Robert kept battling. He married, had three children and fought to make a good life for each of them. He swore that all his kids would get a good education and never be forced to the mills. 'I'd rather send them to Australia than to the mills,' he said. (Australia was an unknown wilderness in those days, a prison colony at the edge of the world.) One of Robert's sons went on to graduate from Queen's College, Cambridge and became a minister. Robert died in 1860 in the home of his daughter.

The more things change

Robert Blincoe gave evidence in special investigations into child labour in England in 1832. The story of his childhood was told in the newspapers, and the public was shocked to realise what bad conditions so many children worked under. Thousands of children died or were crippled for life from working in the cotton mills of England, often referred to as 'the dark Satanic mills'. There was a campaign to improve the lives of working children. Gradually laws were introduced that prevented adults from employing children for long hours or in dangerous occupations.

Compulsory schooling was introduced in Britain, America, Canada and Australia from around 1870 onwards. Getting into the classroom liberated millions of children from the horrors of factory treadmills. Despite this, it wasn't until the early part of the 20th century that child labour began to be less common in countries like England, America and Australia.

You probably think, that was the olden days and stuff like that doesn't happen any more. Guess what—you're wrong. Kids are still slogging their guts out in factories and sweat shops all around the world. The United Nations says that nearly 153 million children between the ages of five and 14 are working in Asia, 80 million in Africa and 17.5 million in Latin America. Sounds like just a lot of big numbers, but they are real kids—ordinary kids who have a right to a safe childhood.

Childhood in chains

Muridke, Pakistan, 1992

Iqbal's voice dropped to a whisper as the overseer walked past him.

'So, we'll go together then?' he asked as he tied another small knot.

'Yes, tomorrow morning,' muttered Mustafa, 'I just hope no one finds out about it.'

The overseer shouted at them and they turned back to their work at the looms.

The air was filled with dust and tiny flecks of wool.

All day the factory echoed with the sound of the looms clacking as the boys wove rugs in beautiful colours to be sent to showrooms around the world.

Somewhere in the factory, one of the new little boys was screaming. He had hurt his finger and the master had forced him to put it into hot oil to toughen his skin.

If any of the kids complained or were too slow they were beaten or hung upside down as a punishment.

Tomorrow, a meeting was to be held in Sheikupura and Ehsan ullah Khan, the president of the Bonded Labor Liberation Front (BLLF) was going to speak to the bonded labourers who were brave enough to attend. Iqbal knew that he would be in trouble if he took a day off work without permission. The master would probably chain him to his loom again, but he was prepared to take the risk.

Debt slave

Iqbal had been sold into bonded labour when he was only five. His mother was ill and needed money for an operation but she had no one to turn to, as Iqbal's father had left when Iqbal was only a few years old. She borrowed 5000 rupees (about $100) from the carpet manufacturer, but it was Iqbal who would have to pay it back.

From the day his mother took out the loan, Iqbal was forced to work at least 12 hours each day, six days every week, for which he was paid only one dollar per week. When the factory was busy meeting an order, he could be at the loom for up to 20 hours a day and sometimes even seven days per week. If he made mistakes, he was fined and the fine was added to his debt. His mother's health was still poor and more small loans were added to the original one. No matter how fast Iqbal worked, he could never repay the money his mother had borrowed. By the time he was ten years old, the amount he owed to the carpet-maker had more than doubled—it could take him the rest of his life to repay the debt.

Cry for freedom

The boys hurried through the busy streets of Sheikupura to reach the meeting place. It had taken them an hour to get to the town by trolley from Muridke. Hundreds of people were milling about in the square listening to Ehsan ullah Khan talk about the fight for justice for the workers of Pakistan.

Iqbal and his friends could hardly see him above the crowd of grown-ups. They were terrified someone would report them to the factory owner, so they lowered their heads and listened to Ehsan ullah Khan telling them how whole families sometimes worked for generations to pay off small loans, and bonded labourers who inherited their fathers' debts were forced to sell their own children. They were little better than slaves to the people who owned them. 'The Abolition of Bonded Labour Act' had been passed by the government in March of that year. The workers had to join together to make the government keep its promises and fight corruption.

Iqbal had always felt the way things were at the carpet factory was wrong. Now he realised that what was happening to him was actually illegal, and that he had rights he had never dreamt of.

Ehsan ullah Khan looked out across the crowd. Something about the small boy staring up at him caught his attention. As the next speaker took the stage, he made his way through the crowd to the boy with the burning eyes.

'Would you like to go up on the stage and say a few words about how it is for you?' asked Khan.

For a moment, Iqbal hesitated before nodding his head.

'Yes,' he replied in the wheezy voice of an old man. (Years of working in the dusty carpet factory had damaged Iqbal's lungs.) 'I will tell my story, but not just my story—I will tell how it is for the children.'

Everyone fell completely quiet as Iqbal's small voice described the terrible conditions of the carpet-weaving children, and asked for help to end their suffering. It was a short speech and when he finished there was silence. For a moment, Iqbal thought no one had heard him but suddenly the crowd burst into spontaneous applause and shouts of praise echoed in his ears.

Iqbal returned to Muridke that evening, his head full of ideas and his heart full of hope. When the BLLF sent him a copy of 'The Abolition of Bonded Labour Act', Iqbal presented it to his former master as his 'letter of freedom'. He never returned to work as a carpet weaver.

A dream becomes reality

By the time Iqbal was 12 he had moved to Lahore to attend one of the BLLF free schools. On weekends he would go back to Muridke to visit his mother, who worked as a cleaner, and his little sister, Sobia.

Iqbal loved school and worked so hard that he passed two grades each year. He had already decided that he wanted to grow up to be a lawyer so he could fight for the rights of other kids. He was often asked to speak at BLLF rallies. His speeches were reprinted in local newspapers and his reputation as a passionate speaker and a crusader for human rights began to grow.

In the two years after Iqbal escaped from the carpet-weaving factory, thousands of other children, inspired by his courage, made a break for freedom. Human rights groups and labour organisations arranged co-ordinated raids on factories that were exploiting their employees. Over 3000 Pakistani kids were freed from forced labour in carpet, textile and brick factories, leather, tanneries and steelworks. Dozens of factories were forced to close as a result.

Snow, ice and friendship

Lidköping, Sweden, 1994

Iqbal reached down into the soft white snow and scooped some into his hands. He waited till the other kids came out of the school hall and into the playground, took aim and threw it at Erik Rydstedt. Erik let out a whoop and wrestled him to the ground, pushing snow down his collar. The two boys collapsed in a heap of laughter as the other kids gathered around them. Even though Iqbal couldn't speak Swedish, he knew how to share a joke.

Iqbal had been in Sweden for nearly a month but he still couldn't get over how friendly everyone was and how at home he felt. A whole new world of opportunities was opening up for Iqbal. Groups of school kids from Lidköping had already visited him in Pakistan and now he had a chance to see how they lived. Erik planned to come to Lahore after Christmas. He was just one of hundreds of Swedish kids involved in a group called Youth Against Slavery. Along with their teachers they were committed to helping the BLLF in its fight against child labour.

Iqbal had flown to Stockholm at the end of October to speak at a conference and receive a tribute from the International Labour Organisation. He had become an

international figure and everyone who heard him speak
was impressed

In December, the sporting footwear company, Reebok,
awarded its annual 'Youth in Action' human rights award
to Iqbal. He flew from Sweden to the USA to receive the
award, give speeches and to meet with politicians and
famous celebrities. He also visited a secondary school and
met kids his own age. The visit was destined to change
the lives of thousands of people.

Sharing the dream

Broad Meadows Middle School is in Quincy, a suburb of
Boston, Massachusetts. The seventh and eighth graders
had been studying the Universal Declaration of Human
Rights, so they knew how important Iqbal's work was,
but nothing could really prepare them for the impact his
words would have on them. Through a translator, he told
them of his life as a child labourer.

'The carpet owners used to tell me that the rugs we
were making—that were stained with our blood—were for
Americans; that it was the Americans who were making
them force us to work like beasts. I thought, "Who are
these people, these Americans? They must be demons!"
I'm glad that I came here and found you don't have little
horns and tails sticking out at the back,' said Iqbal.

Amanda Loos, Jennifer Brundige and Amy Papile were
in the audience. They laughed, but they felt ashamed that
other Americans were buying the rugs.

Seeing Iqbal had an even bigger impact on them than
just reading about him. Iqbal's growth had been stunted
by his years of hard labour—he barely came up to their
shoulders. The children stood on tables so they could see
him as he sat on a chair at the front of their classroom.

He was so small his feet didn't even touch the ground.

'Carpet factory owners prefer children because our tiny fingers make the smallest, tightest knots. And also because they can control us—they are so much bigger and think they can trick us into believing that they have a right to treat us badly,' said Iqbal. 'If we don't know our rights, it is very difficult for us to fight back—we are so afraid. But I'm not scared of the owner any more—now he's afraid of me!'

Iqbal held up a small carpet knife for the kids to see.

'I used to use this tool in my work on the looms. I want to see the children of my country holding pencils in their hands, not these. One day I would like to be to my country, Pakistan, as Abraham Lincoln was to America. I want to fight to end slavery. My dream is to end child labour for all the children of the world.'

After he had finished speaking the kids crowded around him and each gave him a small gift—bubblegum, stickers, friendship bracelets, hundreds of little souvenirs of his visit to them; even a backpack to put it all in. When he went home to Pakistan, he stuck some of the pictures and gifts that the children had given him on the wall beside his bed.

A bullet can't kill a dream

Amanda came inside and played back the messages on the answering machine. When she heard Jen's message, she felt hot with anger. She grabbed the phone and dialled her friend.

'Jen, that was a really cruel joke—pretending that Iqbal is dead.'

'I'm not joking,' replied Jen. 'It's serious—read the front page of the paper. "On Easter Sunday, 16 April 1995,

Iqbal Masih, 12-year-old anti-child-labour campaigner, was shot dead. He was riding a bicycle with his cousins outside his grandmother's house." Someone opened fire on them with a 12-bore shotgun—one of the cousins was hit as well. Within minutes, Iqbal was dead.'

Amanda clutched the phone and felt tears burning her eyes.

'Amanda?' said Jen. 'C'mon over to my house. I need you here. Please.'

Amanda grabbed her knapsack and ran out the back door. The cold spring air made her cheeks flush pink as she ran down the street. When she burst into Jen's kitchen, she wanted to shout with anger but one look at her friend told her Jen had been crying.

'Oh, Jen,' she said. They folded their arms around each other and cried.

The power of seventh graders

The next day was a public holiday, but 30 kids met at the school along with their teacher, Ron Adams. Everyone held hands for a moment of silence and remembered Iqbal.

They hugged each other and spoke softly about him, remembering little things—how tiny his hand had felt when they shook it, how much fire was in his small body. As they talked about him their anger grew and the fire was lit in them too.

Ron Adams got them to write down their thoughts. Suddenly Amy looked up.

'Why don't we *do* something?' she said 'Something that will make a real difference. Why don't we build a school in Pakistan?'

'What? Yeah, right,' said Amanda and rolled her eyes. 'Amy, you are such a dreamer.'

'No, really. Why don't we build a school for Iqbal? We all know how to write letters,' Amy began. 'And we know how to use the e-mail. Well, I think we should write letters to everyone—to all the other middle schools in America, to senators, to the mayor, to everyone we can think of. Ask for donations. Ask for $12 from every grade seven class in every school. Most seventh graders are 12. So we can ask every class of seventh graders to make a donation—$12 from everyone. Iqbal was 12 when he came to visit us, 12 when he won the Reebok award and he was 12 when he died. It's symbolic—it makes you think of Iqbal.'

The room exploded with excited conversation as everyone offered suggestions of how the idea could be made real.

'Okay, slow down,' said Mr Adams, 'I want you guys to go home tonight and write a letter about your ideas. When you've got it in writing we'll have another look at it.'

'He thinks we're going to forget about this,' whispered Amanda.

'He thinks we're crazy,' said Amy.

'He just doesn't know what we can do,' said Jen. 'Never underestimate the power of seventh graders.'

A school for Iqbal

Amanda, Jen and Amy swung into action. Dozens of other kids joined the campaign. They wrote thousands of letters and e-mails, organised fundraising events and made contact with supporters across America. Seventh-graders from all over the country e-mailed their support, made donations and asked how they could help. The campaign leaders worked weekends and through their holidays. By the first anniversary of Iqbal's death in April 1996 the kids at Broad Meadows Middle School had raised over $100 000. At last they had enough money to open a school.

The kids approached 300 different non-governmental organisations from around the world. Twelve of these replied explaining how they would run a school if the kids chose them to organise it. In November 1996, the children chose a Pakistani organisation called Sudhaar, which means 'hope' in Urdu—the language that Iqbal spoke.

Sudhaar is a small non-government organisation that works with the people of the Punjab—the province of Pakistan that Iqbal was from. By December of 1997, 278 working kids from some of the poorest families in Kasur—a city in Pakistan—were attending the school. They were all between four and 12 years of age and many of them were liberated bonded labourers.

The money that the kids from Quincy raised was used to establish The Iqbal Masih Education Foundation, which pays all the daily operating expenses of the school. The money was also invested so it could go on paying for the operation of the school for years to come. It also pays for a credit program which allows families who have sold their children into bonded labour to buy them back.

The kids of Quincy didn't sit back and relax once the school was up and running—they kept fundraising to keep the dream alive. Their slogan became 'A bullet can't kill a dream'.

Amanda, Amy and Jen graduated from Broad Meadows and went on to high school, but none of them abandoned their commitment to the campaign. A whole new group of younger kids have joined the group, including Amy's little brother, Brian, but the three girls still attend the 'School for Iqbal' meetings which are held every Friday night after school.

In May 1998, Amanda Loos marched across America as part of a global march against child labour. Like Iqbal, Amanda hopes to become a lawyer and stay in the frontline of the fight for human rights.

Joining the battle

Craig Kielburger spread the *Toronto Star* newspaper out in front of him at the breakfast table and reached for the sugar. As his eye skimmed over the page he noticed a picture of a small boy smiling up at him—a boy who had just been murdered.

Like Iqbal, Craig was 12 years old, but unlike Iqbal he had a comfortable, safe life. He lived with his family in a leafy suburb of Toronto, Canada, had his own room and went to school every day. He had thought child labour was a thing of the past—that it had ended at least 100 years ago—but reading about Iqbal's life made him realise how wrong he was.

Craig started reading everything he could find about child labour and giving talks on the issue at his school. With a group of his friends, he set up an organisation called 'Free the Children', and together they started to write letters and organise fundraising events.

Several months later, the International Program for the Elimination of Child Labour suggested that Craig's group should send someone to Asia to investigate what was really going on there. Craig managed to talk his parents into letting him go. A friend of the family, who was from Bengal and spoke Bengalese, went with him and together they spent seven weeks touring Nepal, India, Pakistan, Thailand and Bangladesh.

Craig met a girl in a metals factory who showed him

where her arms and legs had been severely burnt by the hot metals she worked with. A boy from a fireworks factory told Craig that when he cut himself his employers had put phosphorus in the wound so it would be burnt shut. Craig spoke with an eight-year-old girl who worked in a recycling factory in India sorting syringes, with no protective clothing. She walked barefoot over a floor that was strewn with used needles.

Both boys and girls showed him scars all over their bodies from punishments they had received. One boy had been branded across the throat with a hot iron for trying to help his brother escape.

The long road home

Craig met people from across Asia who were fighting for change. One group that had organised a raid on a carpet factory invited Craig to accompany 23 children back to their village. The children had been tricked into working for a carpet manufacturer and taken far from their homes with promises of being given fair wages and good working conditions.

On the trip back to their village the children began to sing.

'What are they singing?' asked Craig

'They are singing "We are free. We are going home," said the translator as the jeep splashed along a muddy track.

One nine-year-old boy, Munilal, told Craig how when he had cried for his mother at the carpet factory, he was beaten. So every night he had spoken to her in his dreams. When they reached the village, Munilal saw his mother in the street and leapt from the jeep and ran to her. She knew him instantly and with a cry of joy she threw her arms around his small thin body. Craig knew that Munilal would no longer have to search for his mother in his dreams, but Craig's dream—to help kids like Munilal—was only just beginning.

A voice for the children

Like Iqbal, Craig is a persuasive speaker. While he was in India, he organised press conferences, attended rallies and gave interviews describing all the things he was finding out.

The Canadian Prime Minister was travelling in Asia at the same time as Craig. He decided he should meet with this kid that everyone was talking about. Craig convinced him that he had to take action. The Canadian government agreed to donate $700 000 to the International Program for the Elimination of Child Labour (IPEC) and set up committees to examine ways of preventing exploitation of children both at home and in the countries that Canada traded with.

Free the Children has grown at a fantastic rate, with branches opening in other countries all around the world, and it has raised hundreds of thousands of dollars to help kids who are oppressed. Craig has become an international spokesperson for kid's rights. From Brazil to Sweden, from Washington to Geneva—where there is a chance to help kids gain a voice and be heard by governments—Craig has been there.

A thousand new Iqbals

Although the carpet manufacturers denied responsibility for Iqbal's death, many people believe they were behind his murder. Iqbal had received many death threats in the months before the shooting because he refused to be silent. No one has been brought to justice for the crime.

At Iqbal's funeral, hundreds of children followed his open coffin through the streets of Muridke. But the children of Pakistan were not alone in mourning the loss of Iqbal. On the first anniversary of Iqbal's death, thousands of Swedish children gathered in the main town square of Lidköping to remember the boy who had touched their lives. Erik Rydstedt gave a speech while other kids from Youth Against Slavery sold balloons to raise money to help the BLLF, which has been persecuted and attacked ever since Iqbal's assassination. At the sound of a trumpet fanfare, the children let their balloons go. The morning sky filled with coloured balloons.

All around the world, kids remembered Iqbal and made vows to follow in his footsteps. In Lahore, a small Pakistani girl stood on the steps of Government House, facing the camera of an international filmmaker, and said, 'The day Iqbal died, a thousand new Iqbals sprang up to take his place.'

6 REBELS

It takes a special kind of strength and courage to swim against the tide—to say 'no' when the world tells you something and you know in your heart that it's wrong—especially when you have to say it to people bigger and more powerful than you. Being a rebel is about saying 'no' to stuff.

Rebels come in all shapes and sizes, but I reckon kids are pretty good at being rebels.

This next story is about a kid who had the courage to say no and wouldn't let herself be destroyed no matter how much tough stuff the world dished up to her.

The kid from the Coorong

The strangers arrived at Bonney Reserve in a big, shiny black car and got out clutching brown paper parcels. Ruby watched them from a safe distance.

'They reckon they're gonna take us to the circus,' said her brother, as he stood beside her.

'The circus?'

'Yeah, what do you reckon?'

'I reckon I want to know what they've got wrapped up in all that paper,' said Ruby.

The Hunter kids lived with their grandmother and their relatives in the South Australian Riverland region. They were members of the Ngarrindjeri people and spoke their own language as well as English. For thousands of generations, the Ngarrindjeri people had belonged to the Riverland where the Murray River meets the sea—the Coorong. Ruby had been born on the banks of a billabong and she loved to climb the big gum trees by the water's edge. She and her three brothers and big sister spent their days playing in the bush around their home.

The black shoes

The kids watched as the strangers opened the brown-paper parcels for them and took out a new set of clothes for each of the children.

Ruby slipped the pair of lacy white socks on and buckled up the black shoes. She couldn't believe how shiny they were. When she stared down at them she could almost see her own reflection in the patent leather. But something about the whole situation was bothering her.

Ruby looked up at her grandmother.

'I don't want to go to no circus, Nani. I want to climb a tree and hide.'

'You got to go to the circus, Ruby,' said her grandmother.

'We're going to have a lot of fun together,' said the lady who had given Ruby the clothes. 'You can have jelly and icecream and there'll be laughing clowns. I'm sure you'll enjoy it, Ruby.'

Ruby looked up and nodded politely but she couldn't help feeling there was something wrong about what was happening. Suddenly she felt too hot in the new clothes. She wanted to take off the new dress and the red coat with its fur collar and run back into the bush—but then a policeman arrived and he and the strangers herded all the Hunter kids towards the big black van. Someone pushed Ruby into the van. Ruby was confused. If they were going to a circus, why was there a policeman there? Why were there bars on the windows of the van? She looked across at her grandmother, standing beside the van, and saw a look of pain in her eyes. Ruby felt an answering stab of fear.

As the van sped away from the camp, Ruby and her brothers and sister looked out through the window. Ruby pressed her face against the bars and her eyes stung with tears. Their grandmother had one hand against the side of her face and the other held out—was she waving or reaching out? The car turned a corner, and her grandmother and the camp disappeared from view.

Driving into darkness

It started to grow dark and the Hunter kids had run out of talk. They sat silently in the back of the van, each thinking their own thoughts. Ruby lay down and put her head on her sister's lap, and the rhythm of the long journey lulled her to sleep.

Hours later, Ruby woke up. She was alone. A bright light was glaring down on her.

'How'd they get that little sun in here?' she thought. She discovered she was lying on a narrow bed in a small

room. The 'little sun' was a single light bulb in the
ceiling. Ruby had never been in a room with electric
lighting before—she was used to sunlight, firelight and
starlight.

She shuddered, even though the room wasn't cold. She
sat on the edge of the bed, staring down at the hazy
reflection of her face that she could see in her black patent
leather shoes. She was eight years old and she had never
felt so alone in her life.

Fighting back

Ruby never saw her grandmother again. Nani's grief was
so great at being separated from all her grandkids that she
died of a broken heart before Ruby had finished growing
up. Each of the children was sent to different foster homes
or institutions, and it was many years before they had a
chance to see each other again. In one afternoon, the
authorities had managed to smash Ruby's family to
pieces.

Ruby wound up in a children's home too. There was
no one to kiss or cuddle her any more. She had to do
everything she was told, and do it quickly or she was
punished. But she never forgot her past. She didn't know
where she belonged any more, but she knew she had to
hang on to her memories.

At 13, Ruby ran away from the children's home and
took to living on the streets of Adelaide. The years that
followed were long and hard and often filled with a sort
of hopeless despair. Sometimes the weight of remembering
was almost too much; but she kept fighting and refusing
to let go.

She was still a teenager when she met the man who
would later become her husband, Archie Roach. Archie's

story was like Ruby's—he'd been stolen from his parents and forced to live with strangers.

Ruby grew up and had two boys of her own, but because she missed out as a kid, she was determined to be a mother to as many children as she could. She has been a foster mother to as many as 12 kids at once. She worked as a counsellor and with homeless kids. Ruby also spoke out to let people know about the bad things that have happened to the Aboriginal people. Both Ruby and Archie became well-known singers and songwriters. Their songs have helped people understand just how important it is to remember the true history of the indigenous people of Australia.

The stolen generations

The Hunter kids weren't the only Aboriginal kids who were treated this way. No one knows exactly how many children were stolen from their parents, but the number is probably somewhere around 100 000. Nearly every Aboriginal family in Australia has been affected by the cruel government policies that tore children from their homes. Athlete Cathy Freeman is one—her grandmother and her mum were also of the 'stolen generations' of Aboriginal people.

For most of the twentieth century, right through into the 1970s, the Australian government tried to make Aboriginal kids forget their black heritage. Officials believed that if the kids were taken away from their families they would become more like white people. But the stolen children refused to forget.

On 26 May 1997, a 700-page report was presented to the Australian Parliament. This report told the stories of thousands of children who had been taken from their families. It was the first step in the battle to gain acknowledgement of the wrong that was done to the Aboriginal people. The fight for reconciliation is not over yet, but people like Ruby Hunter will go on saying no to forgetting and keep fighting for respect and justice.

The kids who said no and refused to forget who they were and where they came from have started to turn the tide.

People talk about kids being rebels without causes but usually they have a pretty good idea about what they're on about. Being a rebel can be tricky. For a start, not everyone likes what you get up to, and keeping the faith can be a whole lot harder than it sounds. Sometimes, rebellions don't turn out quite the way the rebels expect.

The Children's Crusade

25 April 1212—St Mark's Day

Stephen stretched himself out on the banks of the Loire River and stared up at the afternoon sky. It was late spring and the sheep were scattered across the meadow, quietly grazing.

Stephen spent most of his time out on the hills with his flock, but that morning he had gone into the city of Chârtres to watch the procession celebrating the day of Black Crosses. Altars were shrouded in black and priests and people went through the streets chanting prayers and carrying black crosses. The priests prayed for Christian crusaders fighting in the Holy Land. Stephen had heard stories about soldiers from all over Europe who had gone to fight the Mohammedans and drive them out of the land of Israel. Even though he was only a shepherd boy, Stephen longed to join the Crusade, to see the place where Jesus was born and take it for the Christians.

The messenger

The stranger arrived with the evening light behind him. Stephen saw him from a distance, a small figure clothed in black and bent over as if tired from a long journey. He was obviously a holy pilgrim, perhaps a priest. Stephen shared his supper with the stranger—a crust of bread and a piece of cheese.

'Tell me of the Orient,' said Stephen, as they finished their meal. 'Have you met many heroes on your journey? How goes the Holy War?'

'Not well, my son,' said the man. 'The men of France waver in their faith, the Crusaders are straggling back to Europe and there is no strong leader to take up the banner. The Lord needs a hero to rouse the spirit of the people.'

'I'd give anything to be able to fight for Jesus,' said Stephen wistfully.

'I'm glad to hear you say that, Stephen, because I have come to you to reveal your mission,' continued the man. 'Here is a letter for you to take to the King of France. It will command him to furnish you with all you need. I want you to lead the Fifth Crusade—the last Crusade— that will reclaim the Holy Land once and for all time. You are the chosen one who will lead the children of Europe to conquer the infidels. You will not need weapons. Your faith alone will conquer the unbelievers. You will go to the infidels with love in your heart and they will convert to the true faith and become Christians. Because you are pure of heart, you will succeed where all others have failed.'

Stephen couldn't speak. He knelt before the man and bowed his head.

'May I be worthy of this honour,' he said.

Raising the banner

The next morning, Stephen woke on his straw pallet in his parents' cottage and looked around him in astonishment. He knew his whole life was about to change.

Stephen told his parents he could no longer tend the sheep because he had a mission from the Lord, but they didn't believe him.

'Don't you realise that the priest must have been Jesus Christ! How can you argue with the commands of Christ?' he cried, waving his letter at them angrily.

For the next month, he told his story to everyone in and around the village of Cloyes. It was very frustrating— people shouted him down and some even laughed at him. At the end of May, he slammed the door to the cottage and took the road to the city of St Denys. He took nothing with him but his crook and a little wallet that his mother had made for him to keep the letter in. He was determined to take his message to more God-loving people than the peasants of Cloyes.

St Denys housed a famous shrine that thousands of pilgrims came to visit. Stephen headed straight to the steps of the shrine and told the people who gathered around him of his meeting with the man he believed was Jesus Christ. He told them he had a mission to save the Holy Land and that every God-loving child in Europe would find glory by joining him. He was a passionate speaker. Pilgrims abandoned the shrine and came to listen.

Children especially were enthralled. It was children alone who would win the war of the Holy Land. The grown-ups had failed and the kids would show them how.

The Great March

Word began to ripple across France from village to village until every child had heard of the boy at St Denys who would lead them to glory in the Holy Land. In streets and fields, everyone was talking of the boy and his letter to the King.

'God can wait no longer,' shouted Stephen to the crowds who came to see him every day. 'We can wait no longer. We will show you knights and warriors what children can do!'

Thousands of children took up the cry. They marched across France to meet with Stephen, carrying wax candles and with crosses held aloft. Parents shouted and wailed to see them go, but the children believed they were acting under a higher law than their parents—their orders were from God. Rich and poor, boys and girls left their homes and took to the roads. Many had lost their own fathers in the wars for the Cross. Some adults joined in, because they loved the idea of pure young children rescuing the Holy Land. A motley crew of thieves and tricksters also followed, considering children easy prey.

King Philip Augustus of France never saw Stephen's letter, but he heard of the crusade. He was torn about what to do. He thought the idea was crazy, but what if he got into trouble with the Pope if he told the children to stop? What if the crusade really was ordered by God? After consulting with his advisers, he issued an edict that the children should return home. He would not support them in their crusade. But still the crowds of children swelled and went on marching to the city of Vendôme to meet with Stephen.

They were unstoppable. If their parents locked them up, they broke down the doors and rushed to join the processions. They sang and shouted and waved banners. Many parents believed the devil was at work.

Meanwhile, the rumour of the new crusade had spread to Germany. A boy called Nicholas, from a town near the city of Cologne, took charge of the German crusade. Like Stephen, Nicholas was a 12-year-old shepherd. He told of seeing a cross of blazing light in the sky and hearing a voice which told him the light was a promise of his success in the holy war. Many German parents hoped that their kids would lose heart by the time they reached Cologne, but by June 1212 Nicholas had an army of 20 000 children marching up the snowy Alps out of Germany to Italy.

Back in France, thousands of children—most of them no more than 12 years old—were marching across the blazing summer countryside. The kids were hot, thirsty and starving. Stephen reassured them by saying the heat was God's way of drying up the sea so that they could walk to the Holy Land when they reached the coast. But God's plan seemed confused, because the smaller children began to die of dehydration. The road to Marseilles was littered with their corpses. Fights began to flare.

When the young crusaders asked Stephen how much longer it would be, he would always reply, 'Soon.' But secretly he was worried. Luckily, the peasants of the countryside were generous and fed the procession as it passed through their villages, but Stephen had no idea how far it was to the coast.

It took a full month to reach the sea. The children had travelled over 500 km on foot with few supplies, and many had given up or been captured by their parents or thieves. Thousands had died. Thirty thousand children had left Vendôme, but only 20 000 stood on the hill above Marseilles. They sang as they marched into the city, where they were welcomed by the citizens.

A way through the waves

In the early morning, Stephen went down to the shore and knelt before the sea. He prayed that God would part the waves as he had for Moses and that a path would open up and allow them to walk all the way to the Holy Land. The blue sea lay calm before him. Little white waves broke on the beach and birds wheeled overhead. Day after day Stephen prayed, but the waters wouldn't part for him and the children became restless. Some left Marseilles and returned home.

When Stephen was at his lowest, he met two merchants who traded with the east, Hugo Ferreus and William Porcus. They offered to help.

'For the cause of God and at no cost, we will supply ships to take you,' announced the traders.

Stephen was ecstatic. This was the way through the sea that God had meant. It was the miracle he had prayed for.

'All other Crusaders and pilgrims have to pay to go to the Holy Land,' he preached to his followers, 'but we will go for nothing. This is a sign that God is with us.'

But many of the children were afraid of the sea. They had expected to walk to Jerusalem. When the final tally was made of those brave enough to cross the sea, only 5000 children and adults had volunteered to continue the Crusade.

On the morning of their departure, the churches of Marseilles were full to overcrowding with children and the people who supported their quest. Stephen led the assembly down to the docks and his young army boarded the ships singing praise to God. Everyone else ran to the cliffs and watched the seven ships and their white sails disappear over the horizon.

The last of the Crusades

It was 18 years before the fate of the child crusaders was known. In 1230, an old priest returned from the Holy Land. He was one of the adults who had accompanied the 5000 in 1212. He told the people of France how two ships had been smashed to pieces in a storm off the coast of Sardinia and all hands lost less than a week after setting out from Marseilles. The other five ships sailed on to Algiers, only to discover that it would have been better if they had gone down too. Porcus and Ferreus were not just merchants—they were slave traders. When the first ship docked, the children were delivered straight into the hands of African slavers. Some of the remaining ships sailed on to Alexandria, in Egypt, where many of the children were bought by the governor to work on his lands. The priests were sold to a sultan, who took them to his palace in Cairo—much luckier than the children, they worked as teachers for the sultan and his family. Hundreds of the children were taken on even further, to Baghdad, and most of them accepted that they would be slaves for the rest of their lives. Eighteen were murdered for refusing to convert to the Muslim faith.

Although Porcus and Ferreus were not punished for their crime toward the children, they were hung for trying to organise a plot to kidnap a German king.

The German children, led by Nicholas, had no more success than the French. They trudged over 1000 km of cold rugged terrain to reach the city of Genoa in Italy. Only 7000 out of 20 000 survived the journey.

At Genoa, the sea was no more willing to part for Nicholas than it had been for Stephen. Thousands turned back. A small group straggled on to Rome and approached Pope Innocent, who told them they had been deceived but asked them to sign a vow to fight in the Crusades when they grew up. In 1217 he launched another Crusade and the children who had hoped to win the Holy War with love were forced to take up arms.

It was not until 1291 that the Crusades finally petered out and the Europeans left the people of Palestine alone.

Dancing to the Piper's tune

Because the Children's Crusade ended so badly, a lot of people wanted to forget about it. History likes to remember the winners. One way the story of the kid crusaders was kept alive was as the fairy tale, 'The Pied Piper of Hamelin'. For the parents whose kids left Germany never to return, Nicholas of Cologne was a real Pied Piper. But not all kids' crusades wind up as fairy tales.

During the 1960s millions of teenagers around the world organised protests against the way grown-ups were failing them. In France, a huge movement—even bigger than the Children's Crusade of 1212—sprang up in May 1968. School and university students joined with unions and organised a national strike that brought the country to a standstill. Their slogans were 'Be realistic, demand the impossible,' and 'It is forbidden to forbid.'

During the 1960s and early 1970s in Australia and America, thousands of students protested about all sorts

of stuff—especially the Vietnam War. Only a few things changed, but as the protesters grew older they got used to the way things were, and just went on with their lives.

But there's one group of kids in Africa, who refused to accept the way things were and they made everyone stop and listen. Their story is really tough—getting yourself heard can be dangerous—but these kids hung in there and kept at it. These kids shouted so long and so loud that their cry is still being heard around the world today.

Soweto uprising

16 June 1976, South Africa

One cold smoggy morning the kids of Soweto woke up full of excitement. They dressed for school as usual, but over 10 000 of them had no intention of going to classes. All over the township, they poured into the streets and began moving towards Orlando. Some were clutching posters that they had made. In their black and white uniforms they were marching to protest—to take on what the grown-ups couldn't.

Hector Pieterson was 12 years old and he was really wound up. Things were going to change and he was going to help. He buttoned up his school shirt and joined his big sister, Antoinette, in the street outside their tiny house. A shimmer of expectation was rippling through Soweto.

'Soweto' is an acronym for 'South Western Townships'. In 1976 it was South Africa's biggest city with a population of two million people. It was also South Africa's biggest ghetto. Only black South Africans lived there, and under the oppressive system of apartheid they were denied all sorts of basic human rights. Black people weren't allowed to use any of the facilities the white people used—not even sit on the same seats in the parks. They were not allowed to own land, nor were they allowed to travel without having special 'passes'. Even though more than 75 per cent of the population was black, they were not allowed to be involved in any political groups. People who spoke out against the system were often beaten, imprisoned and murdered.

Nearby in the 'white' city of Johannesburg, 1.5 million people lived in an area five times the size of Soweto. A third of the households in Johannesburg had swimming pools, but the black families of Soweto didn't even have running water or electricity in their homes. Black people were only allowed to live in Johannesburg as servants to white people. As far as the whites were concerned, Soweto existed simply to provide cheap workers for the white city.

The children of Soweto were angry—and with good reason. On top of all the other difficulties that black students had to contend with, the government was trying to force the students to be taught in the Afrikaans language. Only 8 per cent of the population of South Africa—all white—spoke Afrikaans. It would be of little use to black kids, who already spoke their own African language as well as English. Afrikaans made it extra difficult for them to learn, and thousands of bright kids began to fail the impossible exams they were set. It was another blow to the self-esteem of the black people, another way of keeping them poor and powerless. The kids were not only determined to protest, they were going to fly the black flag of resistance for everyone to see.

Hector and Antoinette quickly met up with kids from their school. The streets were packed with students— thousands of them. They waved placards that read 'Away with Afrikaans' and 'To Hell with Afrikaans'. Some of the girls danced. Antoinette and Hector joined in the singing and chanting. By nine in the morning the chants of 'Power! Power!' were echoing all over the township.

The day that never ended

The students converged on Vilakazi Street on the border of Soweto. They had only a vague idea of what they would do once they were there. They just knew they wanted to be heard; to let the world know what was happening. The student leaders hoped to make speeches and decide as a group what their next step would be. They never got the chance.

Police officers had spotted crowds of children moving towards each other and radioed to Johannesburg for tear gas and reinforcements. Three hundred heavily armed policemen were waiting in Vilakazi Street. One policeman threw a stone at the students and the kids retaliated by throwing stones back. Within minutes, the police opened fire.

Everyone was dumbfounded. They didn't even run. No one had thought they would be shot for simply protesting. For a terrifying moment, they stood in the middle of the road while bullets rained down on them.

Hector fell in the first round of fire. Antoinette was beside him in a moment, screaming for someone to help them. An older student, Mbuyiselo Makhubu, swept the dying boy into his arms and ran, his shirt stained with Hector's blood. Antoinette ran beside him, crying out in pain and horror, as he searched for somewhere to shelter Hector. There was smoke and teargas everywhere. Students were running in every direction. Some were throwing stones at the police in retaliation and the bullets kept flying.

Mbuyiselo laid Hector's body gently in the back of a nearby car. Hector had died in his arms. Antoinette knelt beside her only brother and wept.

Hector Pieterson was the first child to die in the Soweto student protests. Within 48 hours of his death, 65 black people died as they fought back against the brutal police attacks. During the months of unrest that followed, 300 people were killed and over 11 000 injured.

There is a saying in South Africa that when Soweto sneezes, the whole country catches cold. The kids had triggered a sneeze that would make the whole country shake for years to come. Despite the deaths, the kids kept fighting. They wanted to rename South Africa, Azania— an African name for an African nation. They were going to make things happen in Azania, and not even bullets would stop them. No political parties or grown-ups could claim credit for the protests that followed. Press statements were issued by teenagers, and the black youth movement became one of the most powerful forces in South Africa.

Never forget

The 16th of June 1976 is often talked of as the day that never ended. A day that belonged to children helped bring down and transform one of the most racially oppressive governments in the world.

All through the 1980s, the rebellion continued. No matter how they were punished, the people wouldn't be silenced. In 1994 Nelson Mandela, the black political leader who had spent 27 years in prison because he opposed apartheid, was elected President of South Africa. It was the first universal election (where everyone was allowed to vote) that the country had ever held. The long struggle to dismantle apartheid was finally beginning to bear fruit.

The anniversary of Hector's death is a national holiday for most people. If an event clashes with the day of mourning, it's cancelled. People gather around Hector's grave and remember him and the hundreds of kids who died in the months and years that followed. Hector's gravestone reads:

Zolile Hector Pieterson. August 19. 1963-June 16. 1976

Deeply mourned by his parents. sisters

And a nation that remembers

Time is on the side of the oppressed today

Truth is on the side of the oppressed today

One Azania

One Nation

One People

7 RULERS

KIDS IN THE CASTLE—
PRINCES OR PUPPETS?

KIDS RULE OK?

I always used
to reckon
that being
your own boss
must be the
best thing about
being a king—not having
anyone push you around.
But when I started collecting
stories about kid rulers,
I found out things aren't
like that. It turned out that they
get pushed around like anything. Instead of 'KIDS RULE,
OKAY' it sort of works out as kids rule, no way!

The truth is, the stories about kid rulers are
pretty sad. Being a child ruler means being bossed
around by grown-up relatives—they usually have it all
wrapped up. So if you really want to be King of the
Castle, your best bet is to grow up fast.

Temujin the Ironsmith

Chief Yesugei the Brave stepped out of his tent with a small bundle in his arms. The people of the Borjigin and Tayichigud clans emerged from their tents and gathered around him.

'My first-born—a son,' he announced, holding the bundle out for the tribe to see.

'But what is that in the child's right fist?' cried a woman, as she peered at the red-faced baby.

Yesugei smiled. 'He was born clutching it—a clot of blood the size of a knucklebone,' he said proudly.

The crowd murmured.

'It is a sign,' said the woman. 'A magic omen.'

Yesugei looked down at his infant son. 'Yes, the boy will be a great ruler. I will name him Temujin the Ironsmith. He will rule with an iron hand.'

Temujin's bride

Yesugei and his people were Mongols, one of many nomadic tribes that travelled across Mongolia—a huge country in the centre of Asia between Russia and China. The tribe was like a big extended family that moved from place to place with its horses and goats.

When Temujin turned nine, his father decided it was time to find a bride for him. They rode for several days to reach the Onggirat tribe and Temujin was introduced to a shy 10-year-old girl called Borte. Yesugei and the Onggirat chieftains negotiated the marriage and agreed that Temujin should stay for a while to get to know his future bride.

Temujin watched Yesugei mount his horse and ride out of the camp. He would never see his father again.

When Temujin returned home he found the tribe in uproar. On his journey home, Yesugei had met with a tribe of Tatars, traditional enemies of the Tayichigud. They had invited him to eat with them and share their food. Yesugei accepted; but the food was poisoned and he died three days later.

The Tayichigud quickly decided Temujin was too young to lead them. They moved on, abandoning Temujin, his mother Ho'elun and all Temujin's four younger brothers and sister. Ho'elun had no relatives in the tribe and no one wanted to help her raise her children. At only nine years of age, Temujin had to take responsibility for his family.

They lived like wild creatures along the banks of the Onon river. Temujin fished and hunted, while the rest of the family gathered wild fruit, dug roots and tended the few goats left to them. They were often hungry. Temujin grew fierce and wild. In a fit of rage, he killed one of his own brothers in an argument over food.

Four years went by and the Tayichigud heard that Temujin and his family were still alive. They were amazed that Temujin was skilled enough as a hunter to feed his family. They heard that he had killed his own brother. The new leaders of the clan decided he could be dangerous, and they sent men to capture him. When Temujin saw them coming, he mounted his horse and rode into the woods. It took nine days for them to track him down. His captors decided they couldn't afford to take any chances. They put him in wooden stocks, clamping a heavy yoke across his neck and securing his hands, and took him back to their camp as a prisoner. He was 13.

Breaking away

Over by the campfire, the tribespeople were celebrating.

A huge feast was being served and Temujin's guard kept glancing over at what he was missing out on. Temujin lay on the ground and stared up at the night sky. He was weighed down by the heavy wooden stocks and the back of his neck was raw from where the yoke chafed his skin. As he listened to the laughter from the camp, rage bubbled up inside him.

While the guard looked enviously towards the campfire, Temujin quietly got to his feet. It took all his strength to make his next move. Quickly he swung the stocks at the back of the guard's head. The heavy wood made a dull thud as it knocked the man unconscious. Temujin squatted down beside the body and glanced towards the campfire. No one had seen.

It took only a few minutes for Temujin to reach the river bank. He slipped into the icy water, using the wooden stocks to keep himself afloat. Only his upturned face was visible on the surface of the stream.

It didn't take long for a hue and cry to be raised. Temujin closed his eyes and listened to the sound of search parties beating bushes along the river bank. All night, men with torches moved along the river bank and in a wide circle around the camp, searching for him.

When a flaming torch shone brightly into his face, Temujin knew he had been seen; there would be no escape. He looked across the water and met the eyes of his captor. The man nodded and winked before turning away and heading downriver. Temujin couldn't believe his luck.

Just before dawn, the man returned and waded out into the water. He unshackled Temujin from the stocks and helped him to the bank.

'Here's some meat to give you strength,' he said to the shivering boy. 'I am sorry for how the tribe has treated you. Your father was a good chief and you deserved better than this, but you must know that already they fear you.'

'So they should,' said the boy. 'I will not forget your kindness, nor their cruelty. One day, I will take revenge on them and on the Tatars who killed my father.'

'One day, you will be a great ruler. It has been foretold,' said the man.

The universal ruler

Temujin returned to his family. As he grew older, more families came to join his tribe. When he was 14, he went back to the Onggirat people and claimed Borte as his bride.

By 1206 Temujin was in control of most of Mongolia, and the many tribes that he had drawn together declared him 'Genghis Khan' (Universal Ruler). Two years later, he led his armies over the Great Wall and into China. In 1215 he captured the walled city of Beijing, the capital of northern China, and from there he moved on to conquer Korea. Temujin was a military genius and a brilliant organiser. Even though his armies were small to begin with, he led successful invasions of great empires. After conquering nearly all of Asia, he headed west to invade northern India, Turkey and Russia until he controlled nearly all the land between the Caspian Sea and the Arctic Ocean. By the time of his death in 1227, the wild boy who had fed his family on fish and roots had become ruler of the largest empire in the history of the world.

Heir to the throne

The sun was shining and the fields were thick with wildflowers as young Prince Edward and his entourage left Ludlow Castle. It was 23 April 1483. Beside Edward were the two men he trusted most; his half-brother, Sir Richard Grey, and his mother's brother, Lord Rivers. Behind them rode a company of 2000 men. Ten days earlier, Edward had been told of the death of his father, the king. Now he had to travel to London to prepare for his own coronation as Edward V, King of England.

It was a long ride to London and the party would have to detour through Northampton to meet Edward's other uncle, Richard of Gloucester. Gloucester, as the brother of the late king, would act as regent until Edward had learnt all he needed to know to govern the country alone. After all, Edward had only turned 12 a few months earlier.

Twenty-two kilometres south of Northampton, Lord Rivers set the young king up in an inn for the night and rode back to Northampton with Grey to meet the Duke of Gloucester and discuss Edward's future. At dawn the next day, Lord Rivers and Grey awoke to find themselves locked in their rooms.

Gloucester takes over

The streets of Northampton were crowded with soldiers and footmen. Edward stood outside the inn with his servants, wondering what could have happened to Lord Rivers and Grey. When he saw his uncle Gloucester riding towards him he felt relieved. Gloucester and his men leapt from their horses and bowed low before the new king.

'I have come to protect you, dear nephew,' said Gloucester. 'Rivers has conspired to have me killed, planning ambushes along the road. Your father wished for me to be your regent, so I must protect you from the treacherous men who surround you.'

'But Uncle,' said the young prince in surprise, 'I have

great confidence in my uncle and my half-brother. My mother the Queen has always trusted them and assured me that they advise me well.'

'It is no business of the Queen's to be involved in ruling the kingdom. It is not work for women! As to your servants, they are all traitors,' declared Gloucester. 'Men, arrest them immediately!'

The boy king looked on in horror as all his closest servants and supporters were seized by his uncle's soldiers. Those of the entourage that weren't arrested were ordered to return home. Suddenly, Edward was alone. His uncle appointed a whole new set of servants and guards—none of whom he knew.

'No one but I can protect you,' said Gloucester. 'I am the only one who has your best interests at heart.'

Edward didn't know whether to believe him or not.

Sanctuary

In London, Edward's mother heard of what had happened and knew her whole family was in danger. She gathered up her younger son, Richard, the nine-year-old Duke of York, and her five daughters, who ranged in age from two to 17. Taking what treasure they could carry, they sought refuge at Westminster Abbey. The church would protect them if no one else would.

On 4 May, the young King rode into London with Gloucester at his side. Only 500 soldiers accompanied them, each one hand-picked by his uncle. Edward wore rich blue velvet, but his face was pale and drawn. Gloucester and all his men wore black.

'Behold your prince and sovereign lord!' cried Gloucester to the watching crowds.

Some people cheered, but rumours were rippling

through the streets. Ahead of the royal entourage were four cartloads of weapons. The weapons displayed had supposedly been taken from Lord Rivers and Grey before they could attack the Duke and seize control of the kingdom, but Edward knew it was a lie. He had always been a little afraid of his uncle Richard of Gloucester, and now he knew why.

The Tower

'Your Majesty, I am sure you will be much more comfortable at the Tower than here in the Bishop's Palace,' said Gloucester, smiling coldly. Edward felt a chill creep up his spine.

'I am perfectly happy to stay here, Uncle,' said Edward.

'You may be happy but I do not believe you are safe, my lord. The Tower is much more secure than this place. I can keep a much better eye on you there.'

On 19 May, Edward climbed the long flight of stairs that led to the royal apartments in the White Tower of London. At any other time he would have been delighted to be there, but as he stood at the high windows on the south side and looked across the River Thames, he felt terribly alone. The royal arms glowed in the stained-glass windows, a gold and vermilion design of angels and birds was painted on the walls, and on the floor were tiles decorated with the royal leopards and white harts. It was all very beautiful but the walls of the tower were three metres thick, and Edward knew there was no escape.

A cry for help

Edward was relieved when Lord Hastings came into his apartment with a retinue of servants and a sheaf of papers for him to sign. Hastings had been a loyal supporter of Edward's father and was the only man he felt he could trust. But he was shocked at the unhappy expression on Hastings' face.

'I have news for you, my lord,' said Hastings. 'Today, your Council has appointed Gloucester protector of all the kingdom. There is little sovereign business for you to deal with, for nearly all the royal papers will be handled by Gloucester from now on.'

'What does that mean?' asked Edward, alarmed.

'It means that your uncle is in control of England,' replied Hastings glumly.

'Something must be done to stop him!' cried Edward.

'I will do everything I can to help you, my lord, but your uncle is a powerful man.'

On 13 June, Lord Hastings was accused of treason. He and all members of the Council who were still faithful to the young king were executed. Edward watched from the windows of the Tower as his friend's head was chopped off with a sword.

Edward was due to be crowned in only 10 days, but he began to realise the coronation might never happen. Now that Hastings was dead, there was no one he could trust.

The princes in the tower

Three days later, Edward was lying on his bed and groaning in pain. He had a bad toothache and his jaw was swollen but there was no one who could help him. His uncle had dismissed all his servants. The only attendant that he was allowed was an evil-looking man called Will Slaughter, and Edward was loath to ask anything of him.

There was a knock at the door, and Edward sat up and braced himself. When the door opened and his little brother Richard ran into the room, Edward didn't know whether to laugh with pleasure or cry out in fear.

'Richard! What are you doing here?' he cried.

'Uncle said I was to come to be with you for the coronation,' said Richard jumping on to the bed beside his big brother.

'But I thought you were in sanctuary with Mother!' said Edward.

'Well, she didn't want me to come at first, but lots of different gentlemen told her she had to let me. I'm so glad to see you! Aren't you glad to see me?' he asked.

Edward looked at his brother and felt more afraid than he ever had. Richard was meant to be king if anything happened to Edward. Now both the heirs to the throne were firmly in the power of Richard of Gloucester. All they could do was wait to see what their fate would be.

Occasionally, Will Slaughter allowed them to play in the Tower gardens but mostly they kept indoors. The Royal Mint, a small zoo with lions and leopards and the state prison were also at the Tower of London, and there were often visitors milling around in the courtyards. Sometimes people who came to see the animals would glimpse the pale faces of the princes at the Tower windows.

Richard III

On 22 June, when Edward should have been crowned, Gloucester dismissed parliament and postponed the coronation indefinitely. London was full of noblemen who had come from across all England to see the boy king crowned. Richard ensured that all of them knew that he thought young Edward was unfit to reign. On 26 June

1483, Richard of Gloucester declared himself to be the rightful king of England, and a few days later he ordered the execution of the imprisoned Lord Rivers and Richard Grey.

A nobleman was sent to tell Edward that his uncle had been crowned king on 5 July.

'Alas, if only my uncle would let me have my life, though I lose my kingdom,' cried Edward.

The princes were never seen alive again. No explanations were offered for their disappearance. Rumour had it that the boys were smothered to death and buried under a staircase in the White Tower, but no one will ever know exactly how they died. What is certain is that their uncle was determined they would never grow up to challenge his rule.

Despite all his plans, Richard was not to reign happily ever after. His only son died before reaching adulthood and he himself died only two years after assuming the throne, at the battle of Bosworth Field in 1485.

Two hundred years later, the turret at the entrance of the chapel of the White Tower was crumbling. The then king, Charles II, ordered it demolished. On 17 July 1674, the skeletons of two children were found in a wooden chest at the base of the chapel staircase. The small bones had fragments of velvet still clinging to them. No one doubted they were the bodies of the princes. Their remains were taken and buried under an altar of black and white marble in Westminster Abbey.

Even though neither of the young princes grew up to rule, their descendants still wound up on the throne of England. Their elder sister, Elizabeth, married the king who overthrew Richard. Sixty years later her grandson, another Edward, became the first and only boy ruler to wear the English crown.

Edward VI, boy king

Edward VI was only nine years old when he became king in 1547. Even though he had two older half-sisters, Edward inherited the throne. Until recently, girls were always overlooked in preference to boys when it came to inheriting kingdoms.

Everyone was impressed with young Edward. John Knox described him as 'the most godly and virtuous King that has ever been known to have reigned in England'. His mother had died when he was a tiny baby, but her two brothers had always taken an interest in their nephew. When Edward's father died as well, the elder uncle, Lord Somerset, became his Protector. But the younger one, Thomas Seymour, had no intention of being left out of the new king's business.

One night in January 1549 as Edward slept peacefully, the small spaniel dog that lay at the end of his bed leapt to the floor, barking furiously. Edward sat bolt upright as the spaniel rushed to the door that was slowly edging open. There was the loud crack of a pistol shot, and the dog slumped in a heap on the floor.

A huge commotion exploded outside his bedroom— men's shouts, a clash of steel and the sound of guards running along the hallway.

Edward jumped out of bed and ran to the door. His favourite pet lay in a pool of blood on the threshold while guards stood either side of his red-faced uncle Seymour.

'My lord, it was self-defence,' said Seymour. 'I had

only come to see how well you were being guarded. I am sorry for having to kill your dog—it did a finer job of guarding you than these soldiers.'

Edward knelt beside his dog and rested one hand on its still-warm body. He didn't want to believe that his uncle wished him harm, but he couldn't help but suspect the worst.

Puppet ruler

The next day, Seymour was arrested and charged with treason. His plan had been to kidnap Edward so he could control the kingdom. Whoever controlled the life of the boy king controlled the whole country.

On 20 March, Seymour was executed on Tower Hill in London. But that was not the end of plots and schemes designed to turn the young king into a puppet ruler. By October of the same year, his uncle Somerset was in prison. Although he was later released, by 1551 he had fallen so far from Edward's favour that he was also executed.

The new Lord Protector, the Earl of Warwick, allowed Edward to participate in the ruling of the kingdom a lot more than Somerset had, but at the same time, he made sure his own power increased. Edward made him Duke of Northumberland, and granted him more lands and power.

In October of 1553 Edward would be 16 and the government of the realm would be handed over to him completely, but before his 15th birthday, Edward developed a hacking cough. He was pale and thin and when he coughed, blood came up with the spit. The Duke of Northumberland was desperate to keep Edward alive— so much of his power depended on the young king's favour. He organised a stream of doctors and herbalists to attend Edward, but rather than curing him, they only seemed to prolong his agony. On Thursday 6 July 1553, at six o'clock in the evening, while lightning flashed outside his window and huge hailstones crashed against the panes, Edward whispered his last prayer.

The nine-day queen

Edward had dreaded the thought of his big sister Mary coming to the throne after him. She was a Roman Catholic and Edward was a Protestant. All across Europe, Protestants and Catholics were killing each other in fights about religion and Edward was determined that England should have a Protestant ruler. As Edward lay dying, the Duke of Northumberland encouraged him to write a new will ordering that his Protestant cousin, Lady Jane Grey, follow him as queen of England. The Duke had already organised for his own son to marry 15-year-old Lady Jane.

When her father-in-law declared her the new queen, Jane was horrified. Her cousin Edward had been dead for only a few days and she knew she was not the rightful heir to the throne. It belonged first to her cousin Mary, then her cousin Elizabeth.

'The crown is not my right and pleaseth me not,' she said to the Duke. 'The Lady Mary is the rightful heir.'

Her parents, the Duke, her new boy husband and his mother all argued with her. She must take the crown. Jane fell to her knees and prayed. Finally, against what was in her heart, she wearily stood up and seated herself on the throne.

Nine days later, on 19 July 1553, Jane's father burst

into her chamber and ripped down the royal canopy that hung above her supper table.

'You are no longer queen,' he said. 'The Lady Mary and her followers have taken the city.'

'I am very glad of that,' she said calmly.

On 12 February 1554, Lady Jane Grey and her husband, Guildford, were executed. Guildford wept as they walked in procession to Tower Hill, but Jane held her prayer book tightly and kept her head high.

'Lord, into Thy hands I commend my spirit,' she said in a clear voice as the axe fell.

Glory without power

I reckon the two Edwards or Queen Jane might have grown up to be great leaders if they'd had the chance, but they got caught up in the adult world of power and politics before they were ready. To survive as a kid ruler you either have to be as rough as guts, like Genghis Khan, or else be surrounded by people that you can trust. There's one kid who, with the right help and a strong spirit, grew up to be a wise and gentle leader.

The Dalai Lama

Lhamo sat in the sweet-smelling straw and flapped his little arms. His mother had sent him to the hen-house to collect eggs, but he had climbed into the nesting box and sat down, clucking like a hen and laughing. His big brother, Samten, found him there.

'Come back to the house, Lhamo. There are visitors

arriving at the gate. Stop acting like a chicken!'

Lhamo laughed again and climbed down out of the chicken coop. He was two years old. Though Samten was nearly five, it was Lhamo who led the way in the race back down to the house.

The year was 1937 and Samten and Lhamo lived in the village of Taktser in the north-east of Tibet. The village lay on a plateau and was surrounded by fields of wheat and barley. Bright turquoise tiles edged the flat roof of Lhamo's home, and in the middle was a small courtyard. Prayer flags fluttered on top of a tall pole in the courtyard, for Lhamo's family were devout Buddhists.

The rosary beads

Lhamo was sitting by the fire in the kitchen when the visitors were shown into the room and invited to sit down. Lhamo didn't wait for an invitation to climb into the lap of the stranger who wore a long soft cloak lined with lambskin. He touched the string of rosary beads that the man wore around his neck.

'I have this? Mine?' asked Lhamo.

'I will give it to you if you can guess who I am,' said the stranger.

'You Sera-aga,' replied Lhamo.

The stranger looked across at his companion. 'And who is this man?'

'Amdo Kasang,' said Lhamo.

The stranger nodded.

'And the master who is talking with your parents. Who is he?'

'He Losang,' said the small boy impatiently. 'I have the beads now?'

The three strangers stayed the night with Lhamo's

family and in the morning when they were setting out to leave, Lhamo came running from his bed.

'I want to go too. I go with Sera-aga,' he shouted.

His mother laughed and scooped him up into her arms, apologising to the visitors as she ushered them out the door.

After the visitors had left, Lhamo's parents discussed who they might have been. They knew that a lama (head monk) had recently died at the nearby monastery of Kumbum. Buddhists believe that the spirit of a person is reincarnated after death—the old spirit of a wise person will come back in the body of a new baby—so a lama can be replaced by a child. Perhaps the visitors had been searching for the new lama for Kumbum.

Lhamo's parents were partly right. Sera-aga and his companions were searching for a new lama; but not for Kumbum. They were looking for a new Dalai Lama, ruler of all Tibet. The 13th Dalai Lama had died two years earlier in 1933. At his death a great search began for the boy who would be his incarnation.

Tibet is a very religious country with an ancient culture. Since 1391, the country had been ruled by a succession of Dalai Lamas. Tibetans believe that the Dalai Lama is the reincarnation of the body of Buddha. For centuries, each new Dalai Lama had been found in his boyhood by a group of lamas who were sent to search for him. They followed strict rules about how to discover where the spirit of their new ruler could be found, for they had to be sure they had found the right child.

The test

A few days later, a huge search party of senior lamas came back to Lhamo's house. Lhamo's parents were amazed to think their cheeky two-year-old son could be the reincarnation of the Dalai Lama. They ushered the group of holy men into their small home. The lamas believed that if Lhamo really were the reincarnation of the Dalai Lama he would have retained some memories of his past life. The fact that he had been able to name the men who had visited a few days earlier was a sign that he could be the boy they had been searching for.

The lamas and other officials gathered laid out a number of objects on a flat table for Lhamo to examine. The tiny boy walked confidently into the room. He was no higher than the knees of most of the visitors. They all watched him as he looked at the strange things laid out before him.

The first thing they offered him were two identical black rosaries. Lhamo quickly picked the one that had belonged to the 13th Dalai Lama. Next they presented him with two identical yellow ones. Again, he instantly laid his small hand on the one that had belonged to the previous Dalai Lama. Two small drums were put before him and the boy looked at them carefully. One was a small simple drum of the type that monks beat during prayers; the second was much more ornate, with golden straps. Lhamo looked at each of them and picked the simple one. Again he had made the right choice. Lastly they presented him with two walking sticks. For the first time he seemed hesitant. He touched one, and then the other, before choosing the correct walking stick—the one that had belonged to the 13th Dalai Lama. Later, the monks discovered the second walking stick had also been used by the Dalai Lama, but he had given it to a friend who had in turn given it to the lama who was testing Lhamo.

The monks and officials were convinced. This boy was surely the reincarnation of the 13th Dalai Lama. Many other small signs had been revealed to the monks who had been assigned to search for the boy. With their parents' permission, Lhamo and his brother Samten were taken to the nearby monastery of Kumbum.

The young traveller

Lhamo was lonely at the monastery. He was too little to have lessons, and Samten was taken away by tutors for hours on end to learn to read and write. Lhamo would play on his own—often the same game of making up parcels and then setting off on his hobby-horse on a long imaginary journey. Perhaps he understood what his future would be even though he was so small.

A week after Lhamo's fourth birthday, a party of over 50 people set out on foot and horseback to take him to the city of Lhasa where the Dalai Lama's palace was—a three-month journey.

Enthronement

As the party approached Lhasa, Lhamo took off his peasant clothes, put on the robes of a monk and climbed into a gilded palanquin in which he would be carried to the palace. The roadsides were crowded with people dressed in their best clothes. Horns, flutes, drums and cymbals sounded, and people sang and danced as the new Dalai Lama passed by. Lhamo looked out the sides of his palanquin with amazement. The entire population of Lhasa had come to see him arrive. The air was filled with the scent of incense and wild flowers.

As Lhamo entered the throne room, everyone rose to their feet. The Chief Abbot took his tiny hand and led him towards the Lion Throne. It was made of gilded wood with two carved lions at each corner. Five square cushions, each a different colour and covered with brocade, made the throne over two metres high. When he was seated on his throne, the ceremony began.

Throughout the long and complicated ceremony, which included performances, dances, prayers and blessings, the new Dalai Lama was quiet and paid attention to all his duties. He blessed his teachers and the members of his government, drank sweet herbs from a golden cup, and was presented with a golden wheel and a white conch shell—symbols of his spiritual and earthly powers. The peasant boy was now the 14th Dalai Lama of Tibet.

That day, 22 February 1940, four-year-old Lhamo Dhondrub was renamed Jetsun Jamphel Ngawang Lobsang Yeshe Tenzin Gyatso—Holy Lord, Gentle Glory, Compassionate One, Defender of the Faith, Ocean of Wisdom. From that day, Tibetans would refer to him as Yeshe Norbu, the Wish-fulfilling Gem, or simply as Kundun—The Presence. The kings, government officials and maharajas who came to Lhasa to see him enthroned would know him as His Holiness, the Dalai Lama, leader of the people of Tibet.

Freedom in exile

The 14th Dalai Lama's reign was never going to be easy. Tibet had been isolated from the rest of the world for centuries but in the 20th century there had been continuing invasions from China.

After his enthronement, the Dalai Lama spent his childhood studying the history and religion of his country. On 17 November 1950, he assumed full political power. He was only 15 years old but the people needed his leadership. Eighty thousand Chinese soldiers had invaded, and the people of Tibet were suffering. Their lands were being handed over to Chinese farmers and Tibetans were living in terrible conditions. They continued to resist the oppressive Chinese rule but the invading army violently crushed all demonstrations.

In 1954, the Dalai Lama went to Beijing to try and make peace with the Chinese but without success. The situation got worse, not better, and on 10 March 1959, the biggest demonstration in Tibetan history was held in Lhasa. Thousands of people marched through the streets. The Chinese army put a brutal stop to the protests and the Dalai Lama was forced to flee his country. He had argued for a peaceful resolution to the conflict and for freedom and independence for his people, but now his life was at risk and he needed to continue to fight from a safe haven. Thousands of Tibetans followed him into India, where he set up a 'government in exile'. By the 1990s, more than 120 000 Tibetans had left Tibet to be with the Dalai Lama.

In exile, he continues to fight for the rights of his people. He travels the world, drawing attention to their plight and seeking support from other countries for a peaceful resolution to Tibet's problems with China.

'With truth, courage and determination as our weapons, Tibet will be liberated,' he says. 'Our struggle must remain non-violent and free of hatred.'

In 1989, the Dalai Lama was awarded the Nobel Prize for Peace.

I kind of like to think of myself as a fighter but not a soldier. I don't reckon any kid should have to be a real soldier. Grown-ups should keep children out of their arguments.

As many as 250 000 kids are fighting in wars around the world today in 32 different countries. Most of them are teenagers, but children as young as eight are taking part in some of these wars. Heaps of people who fight for human rights are demanding it be stopped, including Craig Kielburger and his gang at Free the Children.

Maybe the best way kids fight is not with guns

but with spirit. Little but tough—that's my motto. Even if
they can't outshoot grown-ups and only occasionally
outsmart them, kids can always try and outlast them.
Sometimes just hanging in there takes heaps of guts.

Stories about kids and war are always pretty heavy.
These ones are from World War II, which was fought
between 1939 and 1945. A big part of that war was the
murder of the Jewish people in Europe—especially Jewish
kids. More than 1 500 000 Jewish children were
murdered during the Holocaust, just because they were
Jews, as well as 4 500 000 grown-up Jews.

As well as the six million Jews who died in the
Holocaust, five million other civilians were murdered.
Anyone who didn't fit Adolf Hitler's idea of what a
German should be was in trouble. Anyone with different
beliefs and different ways of looking at the world—and
that included kids—was at risk.

Arek's war

Arek Hersh stood in the back yard of his cousin's house,
looking across the fence at the golden fields of maize.

Arek's family had come to the village of Zdunska
Wola hoping it would be safer than their home in Sieradz,
close to the German border. A few days earlier, on
1 September 1939, the German army had invaded Poland.

Suddenly, Arek heard a roar overhead. A German
bomber swooped low over his uncle's house, then another
and another. The noise was deafening. The planes began
dive-bombing the village, dropping bombs everywhere.
People poured out of the houses in panic and began
running in all directions.

Arek ran into the fields of maize to hide.

'Arek, Arek, where are you?' he heard his parents calling in panic.

'Here, I'm here,' he called back, but no one heard his small voice above the noise of bombs and gunfire.

'Arek,' called his brother Tovia. 'Arek!'

Arek leapt to his feet as the planes swooped towards him, firing their guns into the maize. He headed for the road but a family with three children lay there dying beside their horse and cart. Terrified, Arek changed direction and ran back towards his cousin's house. Everything went quiet. The planes had gone.

Slave labour

Eventually, Arek and his family made their way to Lodz, where they hoped they would be safe. But the Germans arrived in Lodz on 8 September 1939. Thousands of soldiers marched into the town in long columns.

Jewish men were kicked and beaten in the streets, and sometimes the soldiers cut their beards off to ridicule them. Jewish families had their possessions confiscated. Arek's father decided to take his family back to Sieradz but they found their home had been plundered. Nowhere was safe now that the Germans occupied the whole country.

In the week of his 11th birthday, Arek was caught by the Germans and forced to dig up the bodies of German soldiers who had been killed in the fighting, so they could be placed in coffins. The bodies were horribly wounded and decayed. Arek felt sick but he was forced to keep working.

Jewish schools were closed and shopkeepers were instructed to refuse to sell food to the Jews. All the Jews were rounded up and forced to live in only one part of the town. Arek's father and brother managed to avoid being taken away for slave labour. They thought Arek would be safe because he was so young, but he was seized in their place and sent along with several hundred older men and boys to a 'labour camp' at Otoczno.

At the camp hundreds of Jewish men and boys were crammed into filthy barracks. They were given almost no food and still made to work 14 hours a day. The men were often beaten and punished for almost no reason. Arek saw men hanged because they had tried to steal a single potato. Sometimes he had to cut down the bodies of the murdered men. Of 900 Jews sent to the slave labour camp at Otoczno, only eleven survived. Arek was one of them.

One day after Arek had been at the camp for several months, the commandant looked down at the tiny emaciated boy. Arek was the youngest boy in the camp and was so weak from starvation that he had little strength left.

'You, I'm sending you home,' said the commandant.

The Lodz ghetto

Arek was happy to be back with his mother, but their troubles were not over. On 14 August 1942, at eight in the morning, the Jews of Sieradz were rounded up again. Only those that were useful would be taken to labour camps. For the rest, certain death lay ahead in the terrible concentration camps and death camps that had been built throughout Poland. Arek prayed that his older brother and sister, who were fit and healthy, would be chosen to work. Even his mother had a chance—she was still young. Arek had little hope for himself, he knew he was too small and unskilled to be chosen.

Fourteen hundred Jews crushed into a church waiting

to be interrogated by German SS officers. Although he was only 13, Arek decided he would pretend he had a trade.

'What's your trade?' barked an officer.

'*Schneider* (tailor),' said Arek, drawing himself up to his full height and trying to look confident. The SS officer glanced at his small body and sent him back into the church.

Inside, his mother, brother Tovia and sister Itka were waiting. They too had been rejected. Only 150 of the fittest-looking adults and teenagers were chosen as labourers. Not one of Arek's relatives was among them.

'At least we shall all be together,' thought Arek. 'That is some small thing to be happy about.'

It was hot in the church and after a while, Arek grew thirsty. His mother gave him a metal pan.

'Go and ask the guard for water,' she said.

As he approached the gate an SS officer called out to him.

'Boy, what are you?' he shouted.

'A tailor,' replied Arek, without thinking why he was asked.

'Out!' bawled the officer.

Before Arek realised what was happening, he found himself standing with the 150 people who were to be saved. He was horrified. They were marched away from the church.

Arek spent the long night crying. Everyone tried to assure him that his family would be safe at another camp but Arek had seen enough at Otoczno to know that the Germans showed no mercy. Later he discovered that everyone who had stayed behind at the church had been murdered.

In the morning, soldiers came and took away

everything that the working Jews carried with them—all Arek was left with were six photos of his family and the metal pan his mother had given him. The next day they were sent to the Lodz ghetto. Seventy thousand Jewish people from all over Poland were crammed into a few city blocks and made to work in all sorts of factories for the Germans. After six months living on the streets, growing thinner and hungrier, Arek found a home in the only orphanage left in the ghetto. The children in the orphanage were starving and they had to work every day like the adults but they looked forward to being together in the evenings.

Arek became especially close friends with Genia. Genia was a beautiful girl with big brown eyes, curly black hair and a warm smile. During the day, Genia worked in a leather factory; at night Arek would sit with her as she told stories to the younger children in the orphanage. She loved to take care of the smallest kids. Like Arek, Genia had lost all her family.

In August 1944, the Lodz ghetto was marked for destruction. The Germans were losing the war but they were still determined to destroy the Jews. The people of the ghetto were to be rounded up and taken in trains to death camps at Chelmno and Auschwitz.

Train to hell

The order came for the orphanage to close and 185 children assembled outside it. They were all small and frail from years of living on a starvation diet. They marched through the streets to the railway station. Arek knew how thin their chances of survival were but he pulled himself together and helped Genia comfort the younger children.

So many bodies were crammed tightly into wagons on the train that the passengers could barely breathe. It grew hotter and hotter. Some people, already weak and ill from years of starvation and overwork, died standing up. A few kind people shared the water that they had brought with them, but there was nothing to eat. All day the wagon rattled on. Genia trembled with fear. Arek stroked her face and took her hand in his.

'It's all right, Genia. I have been to a camp before and I am still alive,' he said as he squeezed her hand tightly. Genia grew calmer, but Arek knew they were heading into darkness.

Auschwitz

Early next morning the train stopped. The children were herded down a long concrete ramp. Beyond lay the camp, surrounded by barbed wire and electric fences. Guards were hitting people and shouting at them. Everywhere was noise, distress and confusion. Arek noticed that the Germans were separating people into two rows. The people on the left were mostly old people and small children, many of them from the orphanage. Arek realised they were doomed. He drew himself up to his full height and tried to look strong. The SS men barely glanced at him before pointing him over to the left. Numb with terror, Arek joined the row of those condemned to die. Suddenly there was a commotion and a scuffle broke out. Instinctively, while the guard's attention was elsewhere, Arek stepped across the line and into the right-hand row. No one noticed.

Minutes later he shuffled through the gates and into the camp—Auschwitz.

Over the next year, Arek was to witness unspeakable

brutality. His friends would die around him. Genia was murdered on the first day, others died of disease, some of starvation.

By April 1945, it was clear to everyone that the Germans were losing the war, but the killing didn't stop. As the Germans retreated from the advancing Russian army, Arek and other boys from the camps were rounded up again and taken on one last terrible journey to the ghetto at Theresienstadt.

Beginning of the end

The train came to a stop and everyone was ordered off. As the guards watched, Arek and his friend Yakub made a small fire and cooked themselves grass. It gave them a stomach ache but staved off their hunger. Afterwards, they went down to the river to drink. For no reason, the guards opened fired. Ten prisoners were killed.

All the boys were suffering from severe malnutrition. Everyone was crawling with lice. Every few hours, another person on the train would die. Sometimes Arek wondered what it was that kept him alive.

All night they stood crammed into the wagons while anti-aircraft guns were fired from the train. They had been travelling for nine days, the place they had left had already been liberated by the Americans, and yet they were still prisoners.

A guard opened the side of the wagon and stared in at the boys.

'It won't be long,' said the guard. 'You will soon be free.'

'What do you mean?' asked Arek.

'Hitler is dead,' said the guard.

Arek could hardly believe what he was hearing, but

next time the train stopped, a young Czechoslovakian policeman offered them bread. When an SS guard went to hit one of the boys, the young policeman said, 'If you touch this child, I will shoot you.' The SS guard walked away. Arek knew they would soon be saved.

Theresienstadt

A few days later, in Theresienstadt, Arek woke to the sounds of footsteps and shouting in the street. Climbing up to look out the window, he saw jeeps filled with Russian soldiers arriving and hundreds of people running towards them. People were dancing in the street. Arek realised he wasn't dreaming.

'Wake up! Wake up!' he shouted. 'The Russians have entered the ghetto! We're free!'

He and the other boys in his hut dressed as quickly as they could and raced out into the street. Arek's heart was so full with happiness his chest hurt. He could hardly talk. One of the other boys came back to the bunkhouse with smoked meat, cheese, butter and chocolate. It was the first time Arek had seen such food in over five years. He ate a tiny piece of chocolate. It tasted even better than he had remembered.

The next morning the Germans were rounded up. Arek went to watch. The Russians had given the Jewish people 24 hours to do whatever they wanted to the Germans. Arek stopped an SS captain and asked if he could have his knapsack.

'But it has my food in it!' shouted the captain.

'We have been starved by you for five years,' replied Arek.

The captain began to argue but a Russian soldier pointed his gun at him.

'You are not the masters any more,' he said. 'Give the boy what he asks.'

The captain glared at Arek.

'If I asked this soldier, he would shoot you,' said Arek. 'But we are not murderers, like you.'

Arek was sixteen years old when Theresienstadt was liberated. In the last five years, he had borne witness to the worst horrors that man can inflict upon man. Most people who live to be 90 never have to endure what Arek endured. Luck, courage and persistence allowed him to live to tell his story.

After the war England declared it wanted to take in 1000 young survivors of the camps and make a new home for them in Britain. Despite the fact that over 1 500 000 children had passed through the gates of Auschwitz and other death camps, only 732 child survivors could be found to take up the offer. Arek was one of them. He settled in England permanently and built a new life for himself.

Eva's story

It was 1944 and the Weiss family had been persecuted and stripped of their belongings; so far they had escaped being sent to the Nazi camps but Eva's father decided he must send his children into hiding. Two of them, Kurt and Neomi, had already been sent to a place in the mountains and the two youngest were hidden in another city.

Eva and Marta were waiting to catch a train to Nitra to stay with a German nurse who would be paid to care for them. They had false papers saying they were the nurse's sisters.

Eva's father took her small face in his hands. She was 12 years old and the eldest of his daughters.

'You are on your own now, Eva. But we can still keep in touch by looking at the stars each night. Whenever you are hurt or afraid, look at the stars. I will be looking at the stars too. I will listen, I will hear you and answer.'

As she stepped onto the train, Eva looked back at her father. His face was tired and drawn. He had worked hard helping the last of the Jewish people living in Bratislava, Czechoslovakia. Eva would cling to the memory of those last words with her father.

Sisters together

Despite all their father's careful planning, the girls were not safe for long. Suspicious neighbours reported them to the police. The nurse betrayed them, and the girls were sent to Auschwitz. They spent seven days packed into a railway wagon, with people dying of hunger and thirst around them before they reached the death camp. When the train stopped, someone hoisted Marta up so she could see through the grille at the railway yard.

'There are big chimneys with smoke coming out of them and fences with barbed wire and lots of guards and towers,' cried Marta.

'Come with us,' said some older children to Eva. 'You can pass for sixteen if you stand up straight. You will be safe if you come with us. If you stay with your little sister, you are doomed.'

'I can't make a choice like that,' said Eva.

'Listen to them, Eva. You must go,' said Marta. 'I can die by myself. You live. Just remember this day and say kaddish [a memorial prayer] for me. Tell Mama and Papa too—so they can say kaddish too. You must live.'

But as Eva turned to go, Marta tugged her skirt. 'I'm frightened,' she said softly.

Eva looked at the small girl and took a breath.

'I won't leave you. From now on we'll never be apart,' she said.

Eva kept her promise to Marta. Even though they were starved, beaten and tortured, Marta and Eva managed to stay together.

They were taken to the children's camp where all night, the sound of children crying echoed through the barracks. And every night, though Eva thought it might be her last, she spoke to her father through the stars. She told him what was happening to her—of her fears, her worries, of the unspeakably cruel things that were done to the children in the death camp.

Death and remembrance

Every day, groups of children were rounded up to be taken away for horrific medical experiments. Many of them never returned. One day, a five-year-old boy turned to Eva as he was about to be led away.

'Please remember today and say *kaddish* after me,' he whispered, knowing that he was about to die.

'But I don't know what date it is!' she cried. 'I have to know what day it is to say *kaddish* for you.'

The boy's face crumpled with distress. Eva reached out to him and suddenly, she saw the number that the Germans had tattooed into the flesh of her arm. Every member of the camp, even the children, had been branded with a number to identify them.

'You know what?' she said. 'My number will be your *kaddish*.'

The boy looked back at Eva and smiled as he was led away. Eva bowed her head and prayed for him.

The courage of love

When the Russians finally liberated the camp, they talked of taking all the children back to Russia with them. Terrified, Eva and Marta ran away. They were determined to get back to their parents.

It took months of travelling through war-torn Poland and Czechoslovakia to reach Bratislava again. Eva and Marta arrived back in their home town on a Sabbath morning. As they reached the gate of their house, their father and brother were returning from the synagogue. Even though Eva's head had been shaved, even though she was little more than a skeleton, her father knew her immediately.

Eva's family took her to live in Australia in 1948. When she grew up, she married, had five children of her own and tried to rebuild what had been lost. Yet though more than 50 years have passed, Eva still says *kaddish* for the small boy who was murdered in Auschwitz.

Some of the things that happened to Jewish kids are so bad, it's hard to talk about them. These things never should have happened, but they did, and because they did, they should never be forgotten. Even when remembering stuff is painful, it's important to do it. If we keep remembering, maybe we can make sure the bad things never happen again.

Although six million European Jews died in the death camps during the war, some escaped. Some managed to leave Europe, some stayed in hiding and some joined partisan movements and fought back against the Nazis.

Freight train at Opatova

'Twelve minutes,' said Batko. 'It takes twelve minutes from when we hear them to when they reach the bend. That's how long we have to set it up. Paul, you can be my helper for this one.'

'Yes sir,' said Paul, swallowing hard. He was 15 years old and this was his first mission with the local partisans, near Trencin in Slovakia. They were a tough group of men who sabotaged the Nazis and Batko was their leader.

'The trick is to blow just one section of the track— right on the bend,' continued Batko. 'If we do it properly, it will derail the whole train and drag it down the embankment. Maximum damage with minimum fuss.'

All day, they lay on the hill and watched the freight trains, laden with soldiers, pass along the line. They were waiting for the cover of darkness so they could get to work. By evening, rain was pouring down. While the other men covered them with rifles, Batko and Paul crossed a flat muddy field and hid in a ditch under the rail embankment, listening hard. The rain was so heavy it would muffle the sound of the approaching train. They wouldn't have 12 minutes to mine the line—more like five. Batko placed two boxes of TNT under the rails and linked the cords to the TNT.

'Detonators,' he said.

Paul opened the thick leather pouch he wore at his waist. Nestled in the soft cotton padding were more than a dozen copper detonators. He drew out two caps.

'Okay Paul, now run,' said Batko as the sound of the train grew louder. Paul spun around to follow him and the contents of the pouch scattered onto the ground—he had forgotten to shut it properly. His heart sank. Without the caps, there would be no more chances to blow up the lines—this was their entire supply. With the lights of the engine bearing down on top of him, he scrambled around in the rain, shoving the caps into his pockets, then he picked up his rifle and ran.

Paul stumbled down the embankment and onto the open muddy field that lay between the railway line and the forest. Fifty metres from the line he realised the train was about to pass over the detonators. He threw himself down in the sticky grey mud. As he fell, the TNT blew. Shards of metal flew over his head, some of them digging their jagged edges into the mud around him. Paul looked back over his shoulder to see the entire front of the train lurching down the embankment. He could feel the vibrations of crunching metal as the rear railcars slammed against the wreck of the front carriage.

Paul leapt to his feet and ran again. A bright white flare exploded overhead, and bullets whizzed around his head as the Germans opened fire on the field with machine guns. Paul dived down into the mud again. When the flare burned out, he was up and running again, a moving lump of mud.

Finally, he met up with the squad in the forest.

'Where's that Jewish kid who lost my detonators?' roared Batko. He was pulling his revolver out of its holster. 'He lost the lot, every last detonator, I saw the pouch fly open. I'm gonna get rid of that kid.'

Paul stepped forward, unrecognisable in his shroud of mud. Silently, he plunged his hand into his pockets and pulled out a fistful of detonators. Batko blinked and leaped backwards. The whole squad dived for cover. One squeeze of the caps and Paul would blow himself sky-high. Suddenly, Batko laughed.

'Okay, kid—you live again,' he said.

Paul was to become an expert in derailing trains, an

essential member of the Batko demolition squad. After the war, he went to live in the United States, where he became an authority in computers.

Thousands of kids across Europe escaped to the woods, like Paul, and joined the partisan groups. They lived in the forests making their camps amongst the trees, covering their tracks wherever they went. Every day they worked at blowing up bridges, derailing troop trains, cutting communication wires or nursing other partisans—the faces of those they had lost were always before them.

A light in the darkness

After the war, some Holocaust survivors returned to their home towns. Some went to America, Australia, Israel and other countries to make new lives for themselves, but every year, on the anniversary of the deaths of their friends and family, they light candles. As long as people have the courage to remember the dark past and light a candle, there is hope.

Pirates and swingers

It's hard to believe that anyone could have supported Hitler, but millions of people did. Hitler ordered every German child to join youth clubs. The kids wore brown uniforms and participated in events to support the Nazi Party. But not everyone wanted to join.

Most of the Edelweiss Pirates were aged between 14 and 18 years of age, but some of them were as young as 12. They made up their own uniform and wore little metal flowers on their collars, a skull and crossbones, a checked shirt, dark short trousers and white stockings. There were gangs in most major cities in Germany, and every one of them resisted the efforts of the government to turn them into Nazis.

The Edelweiss Pirates hated Hitler and the youth clubs that were organised in his name. 'Eternal War on the Hitler Youth' was their motto. The Nazis tried to break up the gangs, but as soon as the ringleaders were arrested more boys took their place. As the war dragged on, the Pirates made as much trouble as they could. Brawls between the Pirates and the Hitler Youth League were common. In 1944, 16-year-old Bartel Schink was hung as ringleader of the Cologne Pirates. Finally, thousands of the Pirates were rounded up and sent to camps.

Kids who were into jazz hated the Nazis too. They called themselves Swing Kids. They jived, jitterbugged, listened to music from England and America and welcomed Jewish kids into their clubs. Many of them wound up in camps as well.

Despite the threat of death, thousands of kids did what they thought was right—not what they were told. Sometimes with their parents' help, sometimes on their own, they helped Jewish people and tried to right what wrongs they could. The next story is about two kids who risked their lives for what they knew was right.

Courage

Helena Podgorska sat up in the bed she shared with her big sister.

'Stefania, wake up,' she said, shaking her. 'I think there is someone knocking at the back door.'

It was 1941 and apart from one woman, Stefania and

Helena were the only two people left in the big apartment
building. The year before, the building had been full of
Jewish families but since the Germans had invaded
Poland, all the Jewish people had been forced to move
into a ghetto. A third of the people in Przemysl—over
17 000—were Jewish, and yet now they were all forced
to live in a tiny area while the rest of the city felt empty.
At night, the girls would hear terrible screams from the
ghetto. Helena was only six, but she understood that there
was good reason to be afraid of someone knocking on
your door in the middle of the night.

'Who is it?' asked Stefania.

'It's Joseph.'

'Joseph who?'

'Joseph Diamant. You worked for my mother.'

Stefania had been 13 when she went to live with the
Diamants and they had treated her like one of the family.
She had worked in Mrs Diamant's grocery shop for three
years before the family was sent to the Jewish ghetto.

Stefania flung the door open and Joseph staggered over
the threshold. His face and hands were covered in blood,
his clothes were torn and he could barely stand up.

'Please, Stefania, I need shelter. Just for tonight.'

'Of course, Joseph, but first we must clean you up,'
she said. 'Helena, let's heat some water and get some
cloths so we can dress these wounds.'

Together she and Helena cleaned him and put
ointment on his countless scratches and bruises.

'I slipped under the fence of the ghetto today to visit
you but I couldn't find anyone,' said Stefania as she wiped
the blood from his face. 'What has happened?'

'They've all been murdered or deported to the camps,
Stefania. My brother Henek and I, when they came to
take us, we made a pact that we would commit suicide by

jumping off the train. I wanted to die, Stefania but I am alive thanks to you.'

'Me?' exclaimed Stefania.

'Yes, you. That loaf of bread you gave me the last time you visited—I put it inside my shirt. When I jumped from the car I saw a telegraph pole with a long spike sticking out rushing towards me. I thought, "Right, this is it," and I blacked out. But when I came to I was lying on the ground, my shirt had a big tear in it, and the bread—it was torn open. I think I broke a little bone in my chest but that is all. Your bread saved my life.'

Stefania began to cry.

'Oh Joseph,' she said, 'I couldn't save your brother Isaac.'

Joseph went pale.

She took his hand and told her story. After Mr and Mrs Diamant had been sent to Auschwitz, Isaac was sent to the labour camp in nearby Lvov. Stefania went to visit him and together they had dreamt up a harebrained plan. Isaac would dress in clothes that Stefania had smuggled in to him and wait by the side of the camp. At an appointed time, Stefania would be standing on the nearest corner. He was to scale the fence and run to her. 'If you are with me, we can just disappear into the crowd. I will say you are my brother.'

But the trolley-car Stefania was travelling on was held up.

'I was so late. I was too late,' wept Stefania. 'When I got to the camp, they told me he was dead. He saw a woman that looked like me and ran to her, and she turned him over to the police. I am so sorry, Joseph. I came to tell you, but when I got back to the ghetto everyone was gone!'

Joseph looked pale and exhausted. He rested one hand on Stefania's shoulder.

'You tried, Stefania. You are a brave girl, my friend. You risked your life. Now you risk it again. No one else will take me in. They are too afraid. All my Polish friends have turned me away. If you could let me stay just this one night, maybe tomorrow I will have the strength to search for a hiding place.'

Stefania nodded in mute agreement.

Joseph's clothes were bloodied and torn, so Stefania lent him some of her clothes.

Little Helena clapped her hands and laughed when Joseph emerged from the bedroom in one of Stefania's long flannel nightgowns.

'Now I see two Stefanias!' she giggled, and the three of them laughed.

The hiding place

The next day Joseph was too sick to leave. Helena had to be the scout who would listen to hear if anyone was coming, especially the other woman who lived in the building. She would run into the bedroom and help Stefania hide Joseph under the bed. The girls got used to hiding Joseph and when he brought a friend, Danuta, back with him they didn't hesitate to take her in too. Soon Joseph's brother Henek, who had also survived leaping from the train, joined them as well.

They worked hard at helping Jews. Stefania had a job in a factory and used all the money she could spare to buy food for Joseph and Danuta to smuggle into the ghetto. She even traded her dresses for milk and butter.

One night, Joseph told Stefania the ghetto was about to be completely destroyed. They agreed they must try to rescue as many people as they could, but how? There was no more room in the apartment to hide anyone.

Stefania knew she had to find somewhere else for

them all to live. The task seemed daunting, but a voice inside her told her she would succeed. By a miracle she found exactly what they needed—a cottage with two rooms in the front and rear and a big attic. Helena rolled around the floor and laughed with joy when she saw the place.

'It's perfect,' she exclaimed. 'We can hide everyone here!'

By the time Helena turned seven, there were six Jewish friends to sing her happy birthday, including two children. The fathers of the children were to arrive soon after. 'They can only kill us once for hiding Jews, not ten times. As long as we can fit them in, we may as well,' said Stefania. Helena nodded in agreement.

The plan was for the two men to be smuggled from the ghetto by a postman – but on the day they were to arrive at the cottage, a group of German and Polish policemen began patrolling the street.

'Perhaps today is the day I will be killed,' thought Stefania.

Stefania went to the church and prayed. When she came home, the fathers had arrived safely. Luckily, the postman had got lost on the way to Stefania's house and he was so late that the policemen had left by the time he arrived.

Eating words

Helena grew used to passing notes between Stefania and the last of the Jews in the ghetto. She would slip under the barbed wire when no one was watching. But one day, a gang of teenage boys saw Helena and chased her. Helena couldn't read or write, but she knew the message spelled trouble for all the Jewish people they were hiding. As she ran, she tore the paper into little pieces and ate it piece by piece. By the time the boys caught up with her she had swallowed the whole thing.

'What were you doing in there?' they said. 'Show us what's in your hands.' Silently Helena held them out, empty.

'Turn her pockets out,' ordered the ringleader.

The boys slapped her as she struggled but still the little girl said nothing.

'Rotten little Jew-lover,' they shouted, ripping the pockets off the front of her dress. They beat her and kicked her so badly that she could barely struggle home.

'I told them nothing, Stefania. I told them nothing,' she said as she fell into her sister's arms.

Helena had trained herself so well never to betray the people she was protecting that she became mute for four years after the war ended, and for the rest of her life she spoke with a stutter.

Full house

As the last of the Jews of Przemysl were rounded up and sent to death camps, Stefania and Helena took in seven more people. Now they had 13 Jewish men, women and children living in the attic of the cottage. They built a false wall in the attic so they could all hide behind it in an emergency.

Stefania worked in a factory. There was so much food needed to feed 15 people. She was 17 now and they put her wages up just a little bit, but it was never enough.

Seven-year-old Helena managed the house on her own during the day and did all the shopping. If anyone asked her how two girls could eat so much food, she would tell the shopkeepers that she was selling the extra loaves of bread and sacks of potatoes on the black market. Because of the war, food, medicine, cigarettes and many other things were in short supply across Europe. Shopkeepers were forced to keep their prices reasonable but many people engaged in an illegal (black) market, reselling ordinary goods at high prices to be shipped to areas where the goods were scarce.

After three years—towards the end of the war—a field hospital for the Germans opened in the building opposite the house. Soldiers came and ordered Stefania to leave. For two hours, she ran frantically through Przemysl looking for a house to hide her 13 friends in, but she could find nothing. She gave up and returned to the cottage.

'Run away, don't die with us,' said Joseph. 'You cannot help us any more—you have done what you could. Save your life and save Helena,' he pleaded.

'No,' said Helena. 'No, we can't go.'

Stefania looked from her sister to her friends.

'We won't go. We will pray,' said Stefania. As she prayed, her inner voice spoke to her and told her to be strong and calm.

'Everything will be all right,' said Stefania as she rose to her feet. 'Hide in the attic. Our prayers will be answered.'

Stefania and Helena went downstairs and flung all the windows wide open.

'Miss Podgorska! What are you and your sister doing here!' said her neighbours.

'We're staying. We refuse to be moved,' she replied. 'I'm sick of being shifted around!'

'You're crazy!' said her neighbours. 'They'll kill you both.'

Stefania shrugged. 'We won't go, whatever they do.'

Helena and Stefania cleaned the house, singing all the time. Against all odds, when an SS officer came to inspect the house he said it was all right for them to stay. The army only wanted one room for two nurses to live in.

The nurses moved in and their German soldier boyfriends came and visited them nearly every night. Every night for eight months the nurses and soldiers slept directly under the attic that hid 13 Jews. Every morning, Stefania and Helena watched the German soldiers pick up their guns and wondered if today was the day that they would all be shot. But the Russian army was moving closer to Przemysl, driving the German army out of Poland. Eventually, the field hospital had to pack up and move on.

Liberation

Finally, the Russians came to liberate Przemysl from the Germans. Two soldiers came to Stefania's door, trying to trade chocolate for vodka. Stefania eyed them suspiciously.

'Where are the Germans?' she asked.

'You sound like a spy,' replied the soldiers. 'But look, we've already chased the Germans away. They're never coming back.'

Suddenly, the Jews burst into the room, weeping with relief. They had overheard the Russian soldiers' conversation. The Russians reached for their guns in alarm.

'Don't worry, these are my friends,' cried Stefania. 'Jewish friends. Helena and I have kept them hidden for three years. They are quiet people, good people, the best of people. Please, put your guns away.'

The soldiers gazed at the girls in disbelief.

'Two girls!' said one of the soldiers.

'Not even two,' said the other, looking at little Helena and laughing. 'Just a girl and a half!'

Thirteen people, their kids and their grandkids are alive today because two girls had big hearts, a heap of courage and believed in miracles.

SIGNING OFF AND SIGNING UP

Milo

So that's my swag of stories; but, you know, there are thousands more stories about amazing kids—one book could never be big enough to fit them all in.

In a way, everyone is the hero of their own story. Every kid gets put to the test some time in some way and has the chance to stick with what they think is right. A lot of these stories show that you don't have to be a brainbox or a superstar to make your mark on the world. Never underestimate the power of a kid.

If some of these stories fired you up and set you thinking about kids and the world, there are lots of ways you can find out more. The human rights group, Amnesty International, has a youth network that has branches in secondary schools across Australia. You can find out how to get involved by phoning their toll-free number on 1800 808 157.

You can also get in touch with Craig Kielberger and Free the Children, or the kids at Broad Meadows Middle School, through the websites listed below. These sites can provide you with heaps of links to other groups that are working to help kids all around the world.

Free the Children International
   http://www.freethechildren.org

Broad Meadows Middle School campaign leaders
   http://www.digitalrag.com/iqbal/index.html

Children's World (Youth Against Slavery), Lidköping, Sweden
   http://www.children'sworld.org

INDEX